Loving

Lydia

BONNIE GUERRANT

ISBN 978-1-64258-636-7 (paperback)
ISBN 978-1-64258-637-4 (digital)

Christian Faith Publishing, Inc.
832 Park Avenue
Meadville, PA 16335
www.christianfaithpublishing.com

Printed in the United States of America

Dedication

To Wayne,
who fills each day with love,
laughter and encouragement.
Thank you for believing in me.

1

New Mexico Territory 1900

"Boss, it's a new century!"

The disgusted rancher slashed his hand through the air and stalked away. *If I hear about this new century one more time, I'm gonna explode!* Joseph took several long strides and a few deep breaths, wishing he could control his well-known temper. *I need some help here, Lord. I don't want to blow, but my chest is tight, and my temples are throbbing.*

In a few more paces, he was standing before his black stallion, Titus. He swung a leg over the saddle, turned his faithful friend in the direction of the grazing herd, and loped over the grama grass with the ever-present wind blowing in his face.

Joseph knew his foreman, Buck Hanson, was not being unreasonable. This *was* a new century, and things were changing. The *Clayton Enterprise*, their weekly newspaper, reported new inventions every week. Diesel engines, gasoline-powered tractors, radios, automobiles, electric stoves, household refrigerators, and even adding machines had been invented, and the paper reported that this new century would bring us things that were once considered impossible.

There were changes all around Joseph Banister, but he knew that there were some things that never changed. And the curse was one of them.

Joseph slowed Titus to a walk and forced his mind to forget his problems by enjoying the blessings of the Lord. The rolling grasslands before him had some of the best grazing in these parts, and it belonged to him. He had a large, good-looking herd this year, and soon roundup would begin. He had a comfortable home and was able to provide well for his mother and the ranch employees. He had much for which to be thankful. Why was it that the one thing he could not have was the only thing he wanted most?

Titus made quick work of crossing the plains. Reaching the herd, Joseph recognized the approaching rider as Shorty Lawson, his newest hand. Joseph grinned and shook his head. This was a strange country; a man may never know someone's given name, especially if it were Bartholomew or Herman, but when a man was tagged with a nickname, it stuck. He figured Shorty got his tag because he was a tall man. Joseph, a six-footer himself, guessed Shorty had several more inches on him.

"Hey, Boss, the herd's looking real good," the young cowpoke greeted Joseph. "Some nice-looking calves in the bunch."

"Yep, sure are," Joseph answered, leaning on the saddle horn. "They go to market in a few months, but right now, we got to round 'em up and brand those calves. Then we'll fatten 'em up real good."

"Yes, sir, I...uh...I was hoping to see you sometime today," Shorty stuttered. "I wanted to invite you to my wedding. Me and my girl, Susie, are gitting hitched Sunday."

Joseph worked hard to smile, while his lonesome heart screamed out with the unfairness. "Congratulations, Shorty, I hope you arranged for a few days off. I'll talk to Buck and make sure he's aware of it."

"Thanks, Boss, sure would be nice to have a few days with my bride."

Joseph mumbled, "Don't mention it," and he turned Titus toward home. Home. He wished, but it was no use; only his *mother* waited for him. Sad. At twenty-four years old, his *mother* waited for him. There should be a beautiful woman smiling, standing in the doorway with a couple of rambunctious boys spilling out to see their daddy home from the range.

But that was fantasy.

It was only his mother.

There must never be a wife with his children. He had promised himself and the Lord.

The log ranch house came into view as a great sigh slipped through his lips. *Get yourself under control, Joseph Banister, or you know your mother will ask a million questions that you don't want to answer.* The thoughts just made his shoulders sag even more, but through the years, Joseph had learned how to rally his emotions, especially for his mother.

He guided Titus to the stables close to the house and patted his neck. *Why? Why was I born into* this *family? Why am I forced to carry the burden of my fathers? Enough, Joseph, now get your thoughts where they're supposed to be.* Joseph had given this same speech to himself so many times that it was losing its effectiveness.

A young stable hand reached for the reins of the mighty stallion. "Thanks, Juan. Give him special care and some extra sweet feed tonight. We've been riding the range all day, and he's earned it." With one more pat to the horse's neck, Joseph lowered his weary body to the ground.

"Yes, sir, Boss, I'll take good, good care of him," the young Mexican boy answered, eager to please.

Joseph stretched his tired arms and back as he walked to the house trying to rearrange his black mood. Despite his efforts, when he saw his mother smiling, standing in the doorway, a scowl spread across his face.

"Problems?" she asked, raising her finely arched brows.

And so the questions begin, he thought ruefully. "No," he mumbled as he dropped a quick kiss on her cheek and continued into the ranch house.

"Sit down here"—she patted the leather couch—"and kick those boots off," she said, leaving Joseph in search of something cool for him to drink.

Joseph shook his head, knowing she deserved better. She had endured more than any good, godly woman should have had to put up with from his father and grandfather. He had promised himself a long, long time ago that he would do better than the other men of his family. *Lord, please help me treat my mother with honor and the respect I feel for her.*

By the time Emily Banister reappeared, Joseph sat reclined on the leather couch with his stocking feet propped up on the table in front of him.

"Now that looks comfortable, son." She smiled as she handed him a glass of lemonade.

"Thank you, Mother. It's good to be out of that saddle."

Joseph set his now empty glass on the table and opened his mouth to speak, but his mother held up a silencing hand. "Carlos is filling a tub of hot water for you. Go now, and you'll have enough time to soak and be feeling fresh for supper. Hurry, supper's in about thirty minutes. Maria made you a special dessert."

Moments later, Joseph eased his tall frame into the hot water, once again thanking his mother for insisting on this large tub. He soaked and daydreamed of that beautiful wife coming and washing his back.

"Good grief, Joseph!" his voice broke the silence of his bedroom. "You've got it bad. Get a grip on this. There will *not* be a wife, not now, not ever!"

Each word was spoken louder and louder, echoing in his empty room—empty, much like his heart. To break the spell, he suddenly slipped under the hot water.

"Fences," he shouted as he broke through the water splashing some to the floor. "Fences and steers and cowboys. Work! Think about work!"

Joseph's salvation had been hard work. Since his promise to the Lord, he had worked harder and longer than any other teenager, but as a grown man, the work didn't always take care of the lonely ache in his heart.

The daydreams were the worst. As friends around him married and had children, the daydreams became nightmares for Joseph. His mother only added to his misery by parading every available woman in the territory before him. Time and again, he explained to her that he was not interested, but she seemed more determined to find him a wife.

Later that evening, Joseph hoped his mind would shut down as he laid his exhausted body down to sleep. *Young Joseph cringed as he heard the screen door squeak open and slam shut. His eyes quickly cut to his mother as she rushed to get the remaining dishes on the table for supper.*

"I thought you said supper was ready," Richard Banister bellowed. "Time's wasting, and now I have to sit here and wait for you to do your God-given duty?"

Joseph saw his mother's face pale as his father drew close, stooping a little so he could be eye to eye with her. "What are we waiting on this time, woman? Can't you ever get this right? Honestly, you women have it so easy with these house chores. You'd think that you could at least have my supper on the table on time!"

"Everything is ready but..."

"Shut up, you stupid woman," he yelled, knocking the basket out of her hands and sending biscuits flying. "If there is a but, *then it is* not *ready!"*

When Joseph's mother stooped down to pick up to the biscuits, his father pulled her up by her hair. "Just leave them. They're not fit for the hogs. My mother never could teach you how to cook."

Richard raised his arm back to slap Joseph's mother. "No," the screamed word startled Joseph. He did not realize he had voiced his thoughts until his father stopped, turned, and glared at him. Joseph swallowed hard and knew that his eyes showed the fear he felt.

Joseph's father chuckled and let his arm fly, slapping his wife across the face splitting her lip.

"Do you feel it, Joseph? You see it don't you, boy?" his father grinned. "It is the power that all Banister men have over there women and children. One day you will have it too. God gave man dominion over everything, and we Banister men have this special gift of power."

Joseph's father reclaimed his seat, and after sending his wife a hard glare, he piously bowed his head and began to pray. While he prayed, Joseph thought of his father's words. He did not see his father's behavior as a gift, but as a curse. The curse of the Banister men. Right there, Joseph promised the Lord he would never treat his mother this way. He would never grow up to be like his father. If there was a God in heaven, he would be different.

Joseph jumped straight out of his bed with a cold sweat pouring from his brow. It had been a long time since he had had that nightmare. He propped himself up against the headboard and wiped away the tears and sweat with his sheet. His hand went to the back of his neck, massaging the tight muscles. As his eyes closed, the pain of his childhood engulfed his soul.

He wiped many an unwanted tear from his cheek. How many times and how many tears had he shed for his mother? Why? Why had his father been so cruel to her? She tried hard to please him, yet in return, he hurt her with his harsh words and the back of his hand. Joseph was always amazed at the courage and grace she maintained, never speaking back to her husband, but in the middle of the night, he knew she would slip away and cry, bitter sobs racking her body.

Yes, it had been a long trying week, and Joseph was glad to see it come to an end. The wedding of his cowhand, Shorty Lawson, had begun the week on the wrong note. While Joseph witnessed the young lovers exchange vows, his traitorous heart longed for a love of his own, to find that special woman that would share his life—one he could cherish and nourish, one who would share his dreams and bare his children.

Joseph shook his head. *This war between fantasy and reality must stop!* Some things in life could not be changed, and Joseph must accept that or he would never be able to cope with the life that lay before him. Surely there was more to this life than having a wife and family. He had his ranch and his mother to take care of. *I must work harder, put in more hours, and* not *allow this to destroy the little peace I have in this life.*

Although Joseph had rallied himself early that morning sitting in bed when his feet hit the floor, everything was as before. Throughout the day, he daydreamed, which made him grumpy and fed his temper. As he worked with his men, he was short and more demanding than usual, causing his cowboys to share questioning exchanges behind his back.

When his foreman Buck Hanson approached Joseph with eyes full of concern on Friday, Buck was shut up with a wicked glare. Joseph knew that he should be feeling blessed, but he felt cursed. He knew that he should be feeling full, but he felt empty. He knew that he should feel loved, but all he felt was longing.

By Friday morning, Emily Banister was totally frustrated with her son. He had been so grouchy lately for absolutely no reason. In the dining room, she found a note from Joseph on the table informing her that he would be out very late finishing up the roundup and not to wait supper for him. Now that posed quite a problem for her. She had put off her announcement as long as she could, knowing this was Friday and tomorrow was the day. Joseph had to be told tonight.

Emily chewed on her bottom lip, knowing he would not appreciate what she had done, but in time, she hoped he would thank her. Who was she trying to fool? She loved Joseph more than she could say. It was for the love of her son that she endured the terrible treatment from her husband, Joseph's father. She would do anything for the happiness of her son.

Through the years, she mothered and worried over her only son, but now being a grown man, she feared he would not marry because of her. She tried to show him that she wanted marriage for him, that it would not hurt her. She constantly played matchmaker for him, but he seemed to just barely cope with the situation. It was for this very reason that she took the drastic measures that she would reveal to Joseph tonight.

Joseph could hardly believe his eyes when he walked through the kitchen and saw two place settings. Did his mother wait supper for him? His eyes closed knowing that he would have to carry on a conversation with her.

After cleaning up a little, Joseph and his mother sat down together for their supper. It had been another long, trying day for Joseph with fences down, cows out, and wrapping up the roundup. He wanted nothing more than to inhale his food quietly and quickly and go to bed. He had worked so hard at keeping his temper that he felt he could explode at any time, yet he did not want to subject his mother to his outburst.

After prayer, Joseph had begun to shovel food into his mouth, taking great gulps and swallowing things almost whole. His mother greatly disapproved of such table manners, but he wished to be done with this necessity and excuse himself.

Joseph thought that she must have sensed his mood, and that was why she was so quiet. It was almost an eerie quiet. When he lifted his eyes to check on her, he noted the nervous way she was nibbling on her bottom lip.

Slowly she slid a small piece of paper across the table to him.

My birthday? No, it's not my birthday, Joseph wondered, "What's this, Mother?"

"It's a surprise," she answered with a shaky voice.

Joseph's eyes never moved from his mother's as he picked up the slip of paper, nerves causing his stomach to tighten. His jaw muscles twitched as he opened the paper. Whatever it was, she was definitely apprehensive about it.

When he glanced down, his brows furrowed in confusion. It had a name, a woman's name, on it with additional information:

Lydia Silverstreet
Black Hair Blue Eyes
Age 19 Christian

"What is this?" asking as he gulped some milk.

With an unshed tear in her eye, she whispered, "That's the name of your bride."

"What?" Joseph choked. "What are you talking about?"

"Lydia Silverstreet is a young woman that is coming here for you to marry."

"Now, Mother—" he began, shaking his head violently.

"Joseph," she interrupted, "I know you have not taken a wife because of me—"

"Mother, that is not—" Emily Banister lifted a hand, and with every effort Joseph could muster, he stopped in midsentence.

"I know you have not taken a wife because of me, but I want you to move on with your life, Joseph. I want you to have a family, and I … I want grandchildren."

"No, no, no!" with each word his voice climbed, and his fist slammed the table; all control was gone. "You can't buy or sell wives. You make arrangements to cancel this … this woman!" He shook the piece of paper in her face. The fury in his eyes startled her.

She squealed, "I can't."

"What!" he bellowed coming out of his chair. "You have to. I told you that I'm not going to marry—anyone!"

"Now, Joseph, please sit down and listen to me!" she shouted trying to get his attention. Taking a calming breath, she explained, "I have corresponded with this young woman, and I believe she is sincere. After much prayer, I made promises that will not be broken. Do you understand, Joseph?"

Yes, he understood about promises all too well. But what about his?

"Lydia arrives at noon tomorrow, and we will be there to meet her. I cannot make you love her, but as promised, there will be a marriage."

A FINE DUST HAD SETTLED on Lydia's blue traveling suit. It had been several long days of travel, and soon she would be meeting the Banisters. Joseph Banister. The man she would marry. Lydia gazed out of the train window unaware that she rolled her hands and worried her bottom lip. Not for the first time had she wondered how she had gotten herself into this situation. She leaned a weary head against the side of the passenger car and allowed the rocking of the train to bring the memories of the last few months into her mind.

Lydia followed the starchy, old butler into the family parlor. She had been in the home of her aunt and uncle many times. They lived in a different part of St. Louis than the area in which she lived. The homes here were large and lavish, speaking of the wealth of the families that dwelt there. Uncle Theodore was a banker in one of the largest banks in the city and had been very successful.

The butler led her to the parlor and said that Mrs. Collins would join her shortly. Lydia paced the floor impatient to learn what had bought her across the city. Soon her aunt entered the room wiping tears from red, swollen eyes.

"Oh, child, come here to me. You poor, dear child," she cried, reaching out her arms to the bewildered young woman. "Please, Lydia, come over and sit with me." She sniffed, trying to regain some control.

"Is something wrong, Aunt Edith?" she replied, anxious to learn what had her aunt so upset.

Edith Collins nodded as a fresh flood of tears streamed down her face.

"Lydia, I'm so sorry to have to tell you that there has been a fire," she broke again, sobs shaking her portly frame. "Dear, there was a fire, and both your parents…"

Mother and Father? Lydia's mind repeated trying to make sense of the announcement her aunt had just made. *Oh Lord, how can it be? I was just with them a few hours ago?* Total despair threatened to swallow Lydia. She jumped to her feet and paced back and forth trying to make sense of this. Hot tears slipped out of her closed eyes. Sobs took hold of her small frame, and she plopped down beside her aunt.

The older woman enveloped Lydia in a tight embrace, sobbing herself repeating over and over, "They're gone, they're lost."

Her aunt's words became a steady refrain. *They're gone … they're lost … Mother and Father are both lost …*

And now they are with Me, the inner voice of the Holy Spirit whispered to Lydia's heart. She took a deep breath, and peace began to settle in her heart.

"No, Aunt Edith, they are not lost," she spoke, her voice thick with emotion.

Lydia's words brought tender sympathy to Edith's heart; shock was to be expected. She reached over and patted her niece's hand to lend a little comfort. "Hush now, little one, it will be all right. I know this is a terrible shock and an unspeakable loss."

"No, Aunt Edith, my parents are not lost," she spoke calmly, trying to explain that her parents were safely in the arms of Jesus.

Edith jumped back, "Now, Lydia, I know this is hard, but it will be better for you if you realize that your parents were lost in that fire tonight."

"But that's just it, Aunt Edith, Mother and Father were both saved. The fire was just the means by which they were taken to heaven." A fresh tear slipped down her cheek. "You see, we believe that the moment after we take our last breath on earth, we will be standing in the presence of our loving Savior Jesus Christ."

"Enough, Lydia, I've heard all I care to hear about your religion!" Edith blurted out in total exasperation. "My older brother, your dear father, is dead. While he was alive, I tolerated his religious whims, but I will not, nor do I have to permit you, to belittle me and my beliefs. I am a good person. I believe that is enough to get me to heaven, and I will not have a child, just whet behind the ears, preaching to me otherwise."

By the time Edith finished, her hands were shaking and her face glowed a bright red. She tapped her lacy handkerchief across her forehead trying to wipe away all signs of her outburst.

Taking several deep breaths to calm herself, Edith continued, "My dear, the reality of the situation is that you are now orphaned and have no belongings but those that are on your back. So you will live here with me. I'm quite sure that is what your father would have wanted."

Edith's outburst shattered the fragile peace that had begun to take hold in Lydia's heart. She felt as if she were living a horrible nightmare, and soon the morning light would shine through her bedroom window, and it would be over. She would sit up in the bed and listen to the sweet humming of her mother as she prepared breakfast. After breakfast, they would enjoy a time of devotions.

But one glance at her aunt Edith slammed her back to the present. Her parents were in heaven, and Lydia was left alone. The moment she was about to give in to the grief and loneliness that was engulfing her soul, the precious words from Hebrews soothed her, "I will never leave thee, nor forsake thee." She would get through this with the Lord's help. She found the grace to give her aunt a hug and thanked her for her kindness.

The days that followed had been the hardest that young Lydia had ever been through. Her aunt had taken total control of her life, arranged the funeral services for her parents, purchased new clothes for her, and saw to her every physical need.

But in the ways that her aunt could have helped her spiritually, she fell short and even hindered the attempts of others to help. Because of Edith's bitterness toward the Lord, Lydia was forbidden to attend her own church and forced to accompany the Collins family to their church. The cold marble and glittering gold furnishings reflected the hearts of the people. The services were cold and impersonal, often seeming as if it were a ritual that the parishioners had to go through. The precious truths that Lydia had learned as a child and had applied to her life as a young woman were foreign to her aunt's place of worship.

Lydia missed the warm greetings of her brothers and sisters in Christ. She longed to hear the powerful sermons that were delivered straight from the Word of God, without fear or favor of anyone. She needed the strength that being together as the body of Christ would afford her.

However, Edith would not allow Lydia even those simple things that would comfort her. She openly resented any gesture that Lydia may be practicing any of her beliefs. Lydia was belittled and ostracized because she wanted to please the Lord in her manner of living. During those dark days, Lydia's bedroom became her haven where she could pray and read the Scripture without criticism. She yearned for her solitude and found it harder and harder to be pleasant in her aunt's company.

At first Edith allowed Lydia this time to herself for mourning, but she grew tired of the young woman's mourning. As the days turned to months, Edith insisted Lydia attend boorish dinner parties because she had dressed her in St. Louis's finest and desired to show her off.

When her parents' estate was settled leaving Lydia a virtual pauper, it was decided that Lydia should receive gentlemen callers. Aunt Edith's plan was abundantly clear: marry Lydia off to one of St. Louis's wealthiest young bachelors. Such a union would rid Edith of supporting her niece, while at the same time marrying money and bringing it into the family. No amount of talking could discourage her aunt.

One gentlemen caller after another visited Lydia until she thought she would be sick. Not one had any regard for her Christian manners or morals. She had been poked and prodded as if she were a beef cow taken to market. The young men had the audacity to look her up and down and smile with approval or frown with disapproval, whatever the case may be.

When Lydia mentioned some of the improper attention she had received, her aunt laughed and remarked, "The young men just want to know what they will be getting."

In total despair, Lydia begged the Lord to help her out of this situation and remove her from her aunt's care. Help came from an unsuspecting ally. The young maid that Aunt Edith had assigned her had showed herself to be a Christian with a sweet, godly spirit. Although they were not permitted to fellowship together, the young women exchanged a few words of encouragement if they found themselves alone. Sally assured Lydia that she and her church were praying for her and that the Lord would find a way to help her.

One day when Lydia felt all hope was lost, Sally came in with a page from the newspaper. Sally once again assured Lydia the Lord would make a way of escape and tap the newspaper several times on her vanity for emphasis. Then Sally set the paper down, turned and gave Lydia a pointed look, and tapped the paper again and left. Lydia thought her behavior very unusual until she read an advertisement in the newspaper:

Respectable Young Rancher Looking
for Christian Wife. Write to Emily Banister,
Circle B Ranch, Clayton, New Mexico Territory

She blinked and read the advertisement a second time. It was hard to believe that someone would want to advertise for a wife in the newspaper. She wondered what was wrong with him! Then a small idea began to grow in her mind. Did Sally believe this was an answer to Lydia's prayers? Could God mean this as a way of escape? Why shouldn't she write to this Emily Banister? If she didn't like what she heard, she would not follow through with it. Besides she may be one of many young women to write.

Lydia had no idea what she should write to Emily but decided to give a brief description of herself and of her salvation. She slipped the letter to Sally who saw to it that it was posted. She could hardly wait to receive a reply. She knew it was ridiculous to believe that this advertisement was even on the level, but in some small measure, it gave her hope that one day she could escape the horrible life her aunt had planned for her.

One moment, she believed this was her answer, and the next, she doubted her sanity. Surely no "respectable" rancher would make this kind of arrangement for a wife. And above all, no respectable young woman would go through with this type of marriage. Why, it could even be dangerous!

As the days turned to weeks, Lydia realized that she did want someone to court her and sweep her off her feet. She wanted love, the sweet kind of love her parents shared. The men that Aunt Edith arranged to see her had no concept of this kind of love. And she seriously doubted that a man that advertised in a newspaper would want to court her and love her the way she desired to be loved. But when Sally handed her the letter with the postmark from the New Mexico Territory, her delicate hands shook with excitement.

Emily Banister explained that she was helping her son, Joseph, find a suitable wife. She thanked Lydia for her sweet letter and informed her that she was very interested in learning more about her.

The letter fell from Lydia's hand in pure astonishment. Could this really be happening? The situation with her aunt was becoming increasingly unbearable. Recently, Aunt Edith had been hinting that she would like to announce an engagement between Lydia and some lucky young man. The thought that she would have to live her life with her overdomineering aunt beside her propelled Lydia to write another letter to Emily Banister.

Before the second reply from New Mexico came, Aunt Edith had arranged an engagement between Lydia and Alexander Rowland III. Lydia decided that if she received a favorable response from the Banisters, she would leave for the territory as soon as possible.

Lydia could hardly believe that the train was slowing down. She watched as the houses of the town of Clayton moved past the window of the train. Then she felt the brakes and heard the whistle signal the train's arrival. Her heartbeat steadily increased, even as she tried to calm her sudden case of nerves. She nibbled on her bottom lip and wondered yet again if she had jumped ahead of the Lord. Even so, her travels were at an end, and before her was a new life as the wife of Joseph Banister.

3

JOSEPH WOKE BEFORE DAWN AND saddled Titus. He felt that if he didn't get away, he would suffocate. All the years of hard work and the strain of keeping his desires in check were crumbling at his feet. How could his mother do this to him? Didn't she realize the position in which she was putting him?

There was no way Joseph would let his mother down, yet how could he marry? There must be a way. His mind tumbled one thought after another as he turned Titus toward his favorite thinking place. At times, when he felt he would burst with the pressures of life, he would go to the giant boulder that seemed to pop up out of nowhere. There he would sit upon that rock and think of Psalm 27:5, "For in the time of trouble he shall hide me in his pavilion: in the secret of his tabernacle shall he hide me; he shall set me up upon a rock."

He called it his "praying rock." Things always seemed to be a little clearer out there on that rock. Maybe it was the solitude, or perhaps Joseph just felt he was closer to the Lord there in the beauty of His creation.

This morning, Joseph needed the peace that the rock afforded him. In the dusky dawn of the morning, he sought the Lord. *I'm thankful I can come to you, Lord, and I know you hear me. It seems I'm always in a fix when we meet here on this rock, and I'm afraid it's no different this morning. I have tried all these years to keep my promise that I would love my mother, take care of her, and never treat her like my father and grandfather did. And you've helped me each step of the way. And in so doing, I realized that my father had passed on to me that wicked temper that has the power to hurt others, especially those I love the most. That's when I promised that I would never take a wife and never have a son that would continue this ungodly trait.*

But now, Lord, Mother has arranged a bride for me. Please make her hateful and homely so it will be easier not to love her. I have a plan, and I just need your help to follow it through. In Your name, I pray. Amen.

Had anyone been able to hear the conversation Joseph had with the Lord, they would have thought it humorous. But Joseph was dead serious. There would be a marriage, only to please his mother, but there would be no union. This would assure Joseph that there would be no possibility that another male Banister would be born into this world to carry on the despicable family trait.

Even though Joseph had tried to blot out childhood memories, they had a terrible way of sneaking back into his mind. All this talk of marriage had left his thoughts flooded with unpleasant reminders of his father and grandfather.

For years, he watched as his grandmother and mother were mistreated by their husbands, men that were supposed to love them. He was sure that this sort of abuse must run in the family, being passed down from father to son. No, he could never put a woman—someone that he loved—through that kind of treatment. He believed the Bible taught husbands to love their wives as Christ loved the church. Surely treating a woman like a servant, hurting her delicate spirit with harsh, insensitive words, and sometimes even subjecting her to physical abuse was not Christian. And it was definitely not *loving* someone.

No, Joseph was determined that he would not sin against God in the fashion his father and his grandfather had. There would be a marriage, but he would not fall in love with his wife, and there must never be a union that could produce a son with the family curse.

⸺◈◈◈⸺

Later that morning, as mother and son slowly rode into town, Joseph ventured to ask a question, "Mother, what will happen if I don't like this woman?"

The question surprised Emily. "Joseph, I know you probably think that I have no right to interfere in your life this way," she slowly began explaining, "and if the truth were known, I'm sure it's not the wisest thing for a mother to choose a wife for her son. But if Lydia is anything like she described herself to be, there will be no way that you will *not* love her."

Great! Just what I wanted to hear. It sure sounds like this woman has sold my mother a bill of goods. But I won't be so easily taken in. There must be something wrong with a woman that has to reply to a newspaper advertisement for a husband!

Joseph kept his thoughts to himself. This was going to be tricky—giving his mother the impression that he was thrilled to be married, while at the same time keeping his wife at arm's length. *Oh Lord, what have I gotten myself into?*

The rest of the ride was a quiet one. There was an occasional dog barking as they passed a neighboring ranch and the usual bawling of a new calf after his mother, but no words passed between mother and son.

By the time Joseph and Emily arrived in Clayton to wait for the train, Joseph was a bundle of nerves. His prayer was that this Lydia Silverstreet would be unlovable, making it so much easier for him.

He imagined a buck-toothed, slumped-over kind of woman with a whining, high-pitched voice. Of course, such a wife would be hard to take around in public, but Joseph didn't plan on parading her through town! No, he planned to keep her hidden on the ranch and as far away from him as possible!

Once he had the wagon parked, Emily went into J. W. Evan's Mercantile to make some needed purchases and kill some time. But Joseph had no errands to take up his time; instead, he paced, back and forth, in front of the store until his mother came out and told him he was making a spectacle of himself.

So Joseph took to the streets just walking the boardwalks, hoping the time would pass quickly. Of course, he knew the train was never exactly on time, so there really was no way of knowing how long the wait would be.

Joseph was trying his best not to think about Lydia, the marriage, and all that stuff, but every time he looked around, he saw one couple after another hugged up and in love. He had passed several couples on the walk and noted two more crossing the street. As he passed by the restaurant, it seemed that every table was filled with lovesick *couples*. There were couples on benches and couples in buggies, couples going in stores, and couples coming out of stores.

What's wrong with this town? Joseph pushed his black Stetson back with his hand and scratched his head. This was not a healthy place for him to be! He needed to be around men! And cows, they were safe. Then his mind would not be thinking about a sweet-smelling, soft woman of his own.

It was past noon, and the train was late. Joseph went to the mercantile to help his mother load her purchases, and no sooner had he filled his arms than the train whistle blew, unnerving him completely. He froze and swallowed hard, hoping Lydia Silverstreet had changed her mind.

Emily saw the train pulling into the station and prodded a now very pale Joseph to go meet Lydia. He closed his eyes and breathed deeply, willing his thundering heart to calm down. He dumped his armful of packages in the back of the wagon and plodded toward the train station.

Oh Lord, please, please let her be homely. Let her be a pitiful, little thing, someone that I would never consider falling for. I promise I'll do anything you ask if you will do this for me.

Joseph scanned the passengers as they stepped off the train. He mumbled to himself, "Remember black hair and blue eyes," frustrated that his mother refused to tell him more than that about this woman. Suddenly a tall, broad-shouldered woman with black hair caught his eye. A lopsided grin transformed his worried face as he thought, *Thanks, Lord, she's homely all right. You may have even gone overboard!*

He moved into the crowd of people gathering around the front of the station, and when he was beside her he asked, "Ma'am, are you Lydia Silverstreet?"

"Yes, sir, I'm Lydia Silverstreet."

Panic seized Joseph's heart. That voice did not come from the homely tall woman beside him; it came from behind him. He whirled around to face another black-haired woman. He swallowed hard, stepped back as if he had just been burned, tripped over the first woman, knocking her to the ground, and stumbled through the crowd before landing in the dirt.

The train whistle drew Emily's attention to the depot. Excitement coursed through her as she thought of the young woman that was soon to become her daughter-in-law. After several correspondences with Lydia, Emily knew there was something very special about her. It was Emily's prayer that Joseph would come to love Lydia just as she had begun to love her. A tingle ran down her back in anticipation that from this day forward things were going to change for the better.

The whistle gave another blast, and the engine rolled into town. Emily nudged Joseph with a wide smile on her face, but she could hardly believe it when he dumped his armful of packages into the back of the wagon and walked mesmerized toward the train. She shook her head, hoping that he was just excited about his new bride and wasn't thinking straight.

As she followed Joseph's steps, she noticed a slight hesitancy about him. Once again, she questioned the wisdom in her decision not to share Lydia's letters with Joseph. She hoped that they would enjoy learning more about each other and that it would encourage a love to grow between them. But for now, the only details Joseph knew about Lydia was that she had black hair and blue eyes.

Emily searched the crowd for Lydia as did Joseph. Things happened so quickly that Emily was not sure of the events only that her son was suddenly lying in the dirt. She rushed forward through the gathering crowd to check on him.

Lydia watched as that handsome cowboy tumbled over one of the train passengers, long legs flying and arms thrashing through the air. A black Stetson sailed through the air and landed at her feet. She heard a thump and an "ugh" as the huge man hit the dirt sending a cloud of dust into the air.

The crowd hurried to the side of the woman who now lay flat on her back gulping great breaths of air. Lydia grabbed the cowboy's hat and raced forward, feeling in some degree responsible for startling him. Since she acted so quickly, she was the first to arrive at the big man's side.

"Are you all right, sir?" she inquired with eyes full of concern. "I'm so sorry if I frightened you."

Without opening his eyes, Joseph growled when she mentioned being frightened. He slipped his hand behind his head and winced as his fingers found a goose egg forming.

"Are you hurt?" the voice asked.

"Is he all right?" his mother demanded when she arrived at his side. She knelt down beside him and placed a concerned hand on his arm.

"I think he's hurt," Lydia spoke up.

"Lydia, is that you? Are you Lydia Silverstreet?" Emily asked excitedly, forgetting all about Joseph lying in the dirt. At Lydia's nod, Emily grabbed her up into her arms and hugged her close to her chest.

"I'm Emily," she introduced herself amid tears of joy. "It's so good to have you here."

When Joseph heard his mother say *Lydia*, his eyes flew open just as she embraced the most beautiful woman he had ever seen. *Oh, thanks, Lord! She's the prettiest filly I've ever laid my eyes on. I really appreciate your help!*

Forgetting all about Joseph, Emily stood to her feet and pulled Lydia up to stand in front of her. "Well now, let me have a good look at you."

Joseph used the next few minutes to observe Lydia inconspic-uously. She was a beauty, all right, with shiny, blue-black hair, and cool, blue eyes laced by long, black lashes. *Why a fella could drown in their depths!* The thought shocked Joseph, but still he could not stop his observation of Lydia. Her nose was small and straight, and below were the fullest red lips he had yet to see. *Soft, I bet, soft and sweet. Wait a minute, what am I thinking?*

Joseph's musing caused his heart to sink, yet it began again only to pound wildly in his chest, which only frustrated and incriminated him. He willed his mind to stop its foolish wandering, but it was no use; his eyes continued their search.

She was just a little shorter than his mother. *That would put her about my shoulder height, especially if I leaned into her a little.* Then he heard the conversation turn back to him, so he closed his eyes in a flash and played dumb.

The women knelt down beside Joseph dripping with concern, unaware of his opossum game. He should have felt guilty; he should have jumped up and ran for all he was worth, but he rather enjoyed the attention of two women.

4

BUCK UP, JOSEPH BANISTER, THIS beautiful woman maybe here to marry you, but she is not here to have and to hold! Joseph's square jaw rippled as he thought about Lydia. *Steel yourself to her soft, creamy skin and her sweet-smelling perfume! Remember you've got a plan!* His thoughts helped to get his mind where it needed to be, at least a little.

He heard Lydia say something about her trunk and bags, and his mother suggested that she make arrangements to have them put into their wagon. Before Joseph could open his eyes to assure his mother he would be able to get Lydia's things, Emily was gone, and Joseph was left alone with Lydia. It seemed that his opossum plan had backfired!

"Joseph, are you all right," Lydia asked again, her voice full of concern.

Slowly he opened his eyes and lifted his hand to feel that goose egg on the back of his head. To his surprise and dismay, Lydia's hand joined his, and she checked on the lump too. When he felt her soft touch, a tingle traveled through his hand. His shocked brown eyes locked with bright blue ones, and for long moments, they held each other's gaze.

Emily's voice broke the moment, and Joseph gingerly raised himself into a sitting position. His world was floating just a little, but he wasn't sure if it were due to the knock on the head or the jolt to his heart!

His mother warned, "Easy there, Joseph, you took a pretty hard fall."

"I'm so sorry, I feel that I'm to blame," Lydia whispered, her head bowed.

"Nonsense, my dear," Emily assured, "don't you give that another thought."

Once again the two women had completely forgotten about Joseph. He didn't mind since it allowed him time to watch Lydia unnoticed.

"But, Emily, I think I startled Joseph causing him to trip over that poor woman. Is she going to be all right?"

"Yes, I'm sure she's fine. I saw her moving about just minutes ago. On the other hand, Joseph will surely have a wonderful headache." Emily turned back to Joseph, "C'mon now, dear, let's see if you can stand."

Once again Joseph moved gingerly, raising his body to a standing position, with a woman on each side of him. Aside from his hurting head, everything seemed to be all right. The women tried to fuss over him, but he held a silencing hand in the air; surely he had made enough of a spectacle of himself today. He busied himself with brushing the dust from his shirt sleeves.

"Joseph, this is Lydia," Emily proudly announced. "Lydia Silverstreet, this is my son, Joseph Banister."

When the silence lengthened, Emily nudged Joseph to speak.

Joseph raked his hand through his thick, sandy brown hair, "Howdy, ma'am," he responded without ever looking at her.

Lydia replied hesitantly, "It's good to meet you. I believe this is your hat." She held the dusty black Stetson out to Joseph.

He grabbed the hat, smacked it against his dustier pants, and turned toward the wagon. He hated to be so rude, but there really was no other way to harden his heart against this attractive woman. Joseph sighed deeply and knew he would catch the devil from his mother once she could get him alone, but he must put some distance between Lydia and him. Already he had felt an attraction, and he must work harder than ever to quell all feelings and desires.

⸱❖⸱

Joseph stood beside the wagon ready to lift the ladies up into the seat. He inwardly growled when his mother jumped ahead of Lydia assuring Lydia of the middle position, right next to him! *This is really going to be tough!* Joseph thought as he lifted her into the wagon. *She is so light and tiny.*

Joseph had moved her and set her down so quickly that Lydia became unsteady on her feet, causing Joseph to hold onto her waist a little longer than he felt comfortable with.

"Thank you," she breathed and broke his hold on her so she could take her seat.

Joseph moved to the back of the wagon and secured Lydia's belongings and dawdled with his mother's purchases trying to bolster himself against the little woman with big, beautiful blue eyes.

He was just stepping up into the wagon when he heard his mother mention that the preacher had to leave because of the unexpected death of his brother and would be back on Monday to perform the wedding ceremony. When Joseph heard the word *ceremony*, his foot slipped off the wagon wheel, and he fell forward, cracking his knee into the wheel hub.

He yanked his Stetson off his head, throwing it to the ground, and hollered, "Doggone!" He grabbed his knee and hopped around, mumbling under his breath.

"My goodness, Joseph, are you all right?" Emily questioned.

"Great, Mother, I'm just dandy," he snapped back sarcastically. He snatched up his filthy hat, plunged it onto his sore head, climbed aboard the wagon, and clucked the horses forward.

Joseph was quiet all the way home. He listened to the conversation between his mother and Lydia, wondering why such a lovely woman would need to answer a newspaper advertisement.

Lydia spoke about her train ride and the different kind of people she watched traveling west: older men with big handlebar mustaches, younger men with wanderlust twinkling in their eyes, couples beginning a new life together, and several families. She sat with a young mother traveling to meet her husband in San Francisco who had her hands full with two squirming boys and an infant girl. Lydia became animated when she explained entertaining the boys with Bible stories and even singing with them.

Emily noted, "Sounds like you love children."

"Oh, I do," she enthused. "I hope to have lots and lots of babies of my own."

It took every ounce of determination to pretend he never heard her. *Lots of babies over my dead body! She was cute though, the way she blushed when she thought about what she had said.* Poor Joseph, even his wavering thoughts revealed the battle that waged between his head and his heart.

Emily's eyes wandered from Lydia to her son. Had she gone too far? Had she overstepped the proprieties of motherhood? Of course she had! And she would do it all over again for the love she had for her son.

Her heart had fallen when Joseph seemed to ignore Lydia, but she did not miss the way Joseph noticed Lydia when he lifted her into the wagon, leaning into her hair, inhaling the sweet rose scent, holding her waist to steady her.

Emily's heart took on a new hope when she witnessed the sweet blush that rose over the heart-shaped face of Lydia as the couple's eyes met and studied each other. There was hope! She would do everything within her power to put these young people together, and surely a love would grow.

Dirk Cutter was tired of the trail, tired of the dust, tired of the low-down company he'd been keeping, and tired of running from the law. A slow smile crossed his dark features when he realized he could slip back into life as a law-abiding citizen once again thankful that his alias, Duce Dawson, had done all the law-breaking. Now with a clean shave, haircut, a new suit of clothes, new horse, and honest work, Duce Dawson would disappear.

He milked his smooth face, thinking how he would miss his mustache and his old horse the most, but it was time for a change. That last bank robbery had been a wake-up call, especially when it went sour and he was shot twice in the getaway. It had taken weeks for him to heal, and during that time, he decided to take this step.

He wasn't sure if he could get used to working for money instead of stealing it, but he had to give it a try. However, he had no idea what kind of work to look for or where to find it. He was good with cards, and gambling had always filled in for him when banks and train jobs were few and far between.

Then there was his knowledge of cattle and horses. He was used to riding, and his cattle-rustling days had acquainted him with the animals. Nevertheless, he didn't need to rush things since he had a decent stash of cash saved.

Cutter had just stepped out of Evan's Mercantile when he heard a commotion coming from the direction of the train. He moved in that direction inconspicuously. He stood by to watch since he had never been a man to get involved in other folk's business. In his line of work, it was best to try to remain in the shadows, never bringing attention to yourself.

When the dust cleared, there was a fella lying in the dirt, but he didn't seem to be hurt too bad. Then Cutter saw her. She was the loveliest little thing he had ever seen. Her bright blue suit was the same shade as her stunning blue eyes. Full of concern, she leaned over the prostrate man, and Cutter's eyes narrowed as he tried to discern if the couple knew each other.

He watched the conversation between that beauty and an older woman. Then when the man got to his feet, he all but ignored the tiny woman, yet she left with them. He must find out who she was. He approached several townsfolk and found out that the man was a rancher named Banister from the Circle B Ranch.

Well, it looked like he was going to work on a ranch.

5

JOSEPH GRUDGINGLY HANDED THE WAGON over to Carlos and Juan. He would have rather stayed out in the stable with the animals than to follow the women into the house. He had tried to excuse himself and head out on his horse, but when his mother shot him that don't-you-even-dare look, he changed his mind. He was already in plenty of trouble with her and decided to tread lightly.

He watched as his mother took Lydia by the arm and led her into the house. Apparently she was enjoying this. That was exactly why Joseph must find a way to make this work. He would do anything to assure his mother's happiness, even at the cost of his own.

Joseph tipped his hat back and wiped his head with his sleeve. A slow mischievous smile spread across his face as he wandered toward the house. Despite everything, he was sure Lydia was some kind of woman. Although she was young, she had traveled by herself through several states on two different trains. She sure had pluck!

Joseph stopped on the shaded patio and stretched out on a delicate wrought iron bench. He folded his hands over his broad chest and enjoyed the peace this beautiful garden provided. He took his hat off, set it down beside him, and raked his fingers through his hair, wondering if Lydia knew how beautiful she was. From what Joseph noticed, she had not behaved snooty or high-minded, but it was still a mystery to him exactly why she had answered that advertisement.

He glanced down at his pants and finally noticed how filthy that fall in the dirt had made him. He snatched his new black Stetson off the bench and growled, thinking it looked worse than his work hat. *Women! Nothing but trouble, and now I have* two*!* Thoughts of his mother prompted him off the bench and quietly into his room to clean up.

Lydia sat down in the high-backed chair in the lovely guest room. Emily had shown her to the room, suggesting she take some time to rest and freshen up since the evening meal was several hours away.

Lydia was terribly exhausted, longing for a bath and a bed. She felt a little better now that her traveling was over; although, she would never allow the Banisters to know how frightened she had been when she stepped of that train.

She had answered Emily's petition and later her letters because she was more afraid to stay and marry Aunt Edith's choice of husbands than to marry a stranger. It was pure adrenaline that drove her to sneak out of her aunt's house and on to the train station. Once she was out of St. Louis, the possible consequences of leaving everything she knew for the unknown rushed in upon her heart. Doubt assailed her. Had she stepped out of God's will?

She had shed fearful tears that turned into a prayer for protection and guidance. Although Lydia could not explain it in words, a peace settled in her heart that the Lord had indeed prepared the way for her and was even now walking with her.

She had thought of the children of Israel as they were thrust out of Egypt and into the wilderness. The Lord had made many promises to His children and never had broken even the least of them. Tears formed in her eyes as the memory of her dear mother sharing this story with her many years ago filled her mind. She had shown Lydia the promises in Deuteronomy 31:6, 8 and marked them in her Bible for future reference.

"Oh, Mama," she whispered, "you had no idea how much I would need those promises that you shared with me so long ago." Lydia slipped a lacy handkerchief from her handbag and dabbed her wet eyes.

Once again the memorized words came to her mind as they had on and off during her long journey to the Banisters, "Be strong and of a good courage, fear not, nor be afraid of them: for the Lord thy God, he it is that goeth with thee; he will never fail thee, nor forsake thee…And the Lord, he it is that doth go before thee; he will be with thee, he will not fail thee, neither forsake thee: fear not, neither be dismayed."

A knock at her door brought her back to the present as a tiny Mexican woman peeked around the door and told her in a heavy accent that they had her trunk and bags. She bade them enter, and an older man and a young boy brought in her belongings.

When she was left alone, Lydia's eyes finally scanned the room in which she was to stay. It was so different from anything she had ever known. The walls were white stucco with fixtures of black wrought iron and accented with shades of red. There was a huge four-poster bed with a handmade log cabin quilt in which every strip of fabric boasted some shade of red and was further accented by the red throw pillows. The room had a tall wardrobe beside the door and a dressing screen in the corner. Opposite the bed was a lovely dresser that supported a large mirror. A small bedroom heater stood in the far corner of the outside wall and was accompanied by the two red velvet–covered chairs separated by a delicately carved wooden table.

Lydia inwardly complimented Emily's taste in decorating when she noticed a small envelope propped up against the kerosene lamp on the table. Upon closer inspection, she saw it was addressed to her. She stared at it for the longest time, then reached for it. The handwriting was definitely feminine. Inside was a note from Emily that read:

> Dearest Lydia,
> I'm so pleased to have you here in our home. I have written these words because I do not think I could speak them. I was so sorry to hear that your parents had gone on to heaven. I know that I could never replace your mother, but if you will

allow me, I will love you just as if you were my
own daughter.

Sincerely,
Emily Banister

The thoughtfulness of the note overwhelmed Lydia, and the tears that she had deprived herself began to fall. She slid to the side of the bed and wept until the tears were dried up. Then she lifted her heart to the Lord in prayer. She asked Him to forgive her for the way she had sneaked out of St. Louis and asked the Lord to help her aunt and uncle to understand and one day forgive her. Lydia begged the Lord to help her know His will concerning Joseph and the upcoming marriage and as always to teach her to trust Him with all of her heart.

A knock and Emily's voice brought her prayers to a sudden end. When she opened the door, she gave the older woman a tender hug and whispered a thank you in her ear. No other words were necessary, for they both knew what it was all about.

Emily pulled Lydia to arm's length and explained to her where the outdoor facilities were and that a bath would be in her room when she returned. Lydia smiled contentedly as she passed through the long hall and went out the back door. There was no doubt about the way Emily felt about her, but she wondered what Joseph thought.

Back in her room, Lydia decided not to take her hair down, knowing it would need a whole afternoon to dry. When she had finished bathing, she took some time to hang her dresses in the wardrobe and unpack her bags. Then she ventured out of her room in search of Emily.

She entered the long hallway and took more notice of her surroundings. There were three doors to the left, the door to the outside at the end of the hall, and a set of French doors on the right side of the hall. She was surprised to see that they led to a beautiful patio.

Two sides of the patio were formed by the house and the other two sides were formed by a shoulder-high stucco wall. Wrought iron poles along the top of the wall supported large beams that formed a trellis-like overhead structure. In each of the stucco walls, there was an ornately fashioned wrought iron gate leading out into the yard.

The floor of the patio was some sort of a red tile with a tree growing right in the center of it. Along the walls were manicured flower beds with higher bushes in the corners and several wrought iron benches. In the nook formed by the walls of the house, there was a wrought iron table with chairs.

Lydia had never seen anything so inviting. She longed to sit on each bench and discover something new about this wonderland, but she knew it must be close to meal time. As if her stomach had known her thoughts, it let out a loud rumble.

As Joseph stepped through the doorway of his room, he watched Lydia disappear into the patio. Despite his resolve to distance himself from her, he followed her and stood just behind her as she discovered the lovely garden. He enjoyed watching her study the space and leaned ever so slightly to the side to observe her facial expressions. He was rewarded when her delicate features produced a smile, transforming her face. As she studied the garden, he noticed that she took a wayward strand of silky black hair and twisted it around her finger.

The loud rumble indicating her hunger broke his spell, and he leaned near her ear and asked, "Are you hungry?"

Lydia jumped at the nearness of the voice and backed right into Joseph's large chest. Jumping away from him, her small hand flew to her thumping breast.

"Oh, Joseph, I didn't know you were there. You scared me silly." A twinkle lit her eyes and a tiny smiled tugged at her lips. "I guess we are even now, aren't we?"

How could a tiny tug of her lips do such huge things to his heart, not to mention his sweaty palms? A lopsided smile pulled at his own mouth as he conceded, "Yep, I guess that makes us even." He shook his freshly washed head and reached for her elbow, escorting her through another door off the patio and into the dining room.

Joseph noted the surprised look on his mother's face when he and Lydia entered the room. He sent her a huge smile and seated Lydia, then took his own seat. When he looked up and saw two smiling women, it helped him to return to his senses. The friendly, cordial Joseph must disappear never to appear again! He had to remember his plan. He could not fall for Lydia!

After giving thanks for the meal, Joseph concentrated on eating and tried his best to ignore the beautiful blue eyes across the table. And he definitely steered clear of his mother's questioning eyes. Both females showed their confusion in his mood change, but he could not let that alter his course.

The tension during the meal built with Lydia looking for a way to escape and his mother ready to blow. How had he gotten here? His life up until today had not been *that* bad. So what if he longed for a love he could never have? So what if the future stretched out into a dismal, bleak-looking desert? His life was good!

His mother cleared her throat about the time that Lydia jumped up from the table and grabbed his coffee cup.

"Joseph, would you like some more coffee?" she asked sweetly, and before he could reply, she almost ran in the direction of the kitchen.

Joseph exchanged a stunned look with his mother. She leaned toward him with narrowed eyes and a pinched mouth and spoke in whispered tones, "Joseph, I don't know what's gotten into to you, but I am telling you right now that you had better get over it! From the time that Lydia stepped off that train, you have been a moody, clumsy knothead, and I want it to stop right now! Why, I'm ashamed. Do you understand, Joseph?"

She began wagging her finger, and Joseph knew that was a sure sign she was at her breaking point.

"When she comes back in here," she continued to warn him, "you had better make her feel like she is welcome in this house. I mean it. You had better talk to her."

Joseph knew he had it coming, but there was no way he could tell his mother that it was because of his attraction to Lydia he was doing everything in his power to ignore her.

When Lydia reentered the dining room, her nose was suspiciously pink. She set Joseph's cup down without a word and took her seat.

"Thank you, Lydia," Joseph spoke for the first time since he had offered grace.

Two heads jerked up at the sound of his voice; he smiled a cheeky grin, winked at his mother, crossed his long legs, and took a sip of his coffee.

"Lydia," his voice once again surprised her, "how do your parents feel about your move out west?"

Emily choked on her coffee, and Lydia's fork stopped in midair. Instant tears glistened in her wounded eyes, assuring Joseph that he had chosen the wrong question. When he looked to his mother for conformation, she just bowed her wagging head.

Emily broke the silence, "Oh, I'm so sorry, Lydia. Joseph had no idea. You see, I did not share my letters with him, and he couldn't have known how much it would hurt you to explain."

6

Dirk Cutter made quick work of getting directions to the Circle B. He didn't want to waste any time in finding out who the beauty was and how he could have her for himself. Although dusk was settling on the land, he approached the ranch and sought out the ranch foreman to ask for work.

"No, I'm sorry, uh …," Buck Hanson, the Circle B foreman paused, "what did you say your name was?"

"Cutter, Dirk Cutter."

"Cutter, no, I'm afraid I have all the hands I need right now."

Cutter flashed a friendly smile and reached to shake Buck's hand. "Well, I appreciate your time. Look, I could really use the work, so if you should need someone, I'm in town at the Elund Hotel."

The foreman glanced at Cutter's new duds, and the question appeared on his face even though he didn't ask it. Cutter silently cursed himself for not thinking of the impression new clothes would give the foreman. Evidently, this Hanson fella was a careful man, and Cutter had better remember that for the future.

"I'll keep that in mind," Hanson said in dismissal and turned back to unsaddling his horse.

Cutter felt the man's eyes on him as he mounted his horse, willing every muscle in his body to relax. He was not used to being told *no.* He spurred the horse and turned toward town. This would take a little more thinking time. He had to figure out a way to *make* the Circle B foreman hire him.

He slowed the pinto to a walk and moved his gloved hand to stroke a missing mustache. He wasn't sure he liked the idea of being clean-shaven again. He didn't mind shedding the longer straight, brown hair, but he had really liked that mustache.

When he topped the rise, the wind hitting him in the face, he stopped and turned to face the Circle B ranch. He appreciated the hard work it must have taken to cut the well-ordered ranch from this wilderness. Evidently, that fella he saw lying in the dirt today must be smarter than what he looked.

It would take a few days to come up with a plan, but that made no difference to him. He had time and money (and he knew he could get more money anytime he needed it), but more importantly, he had a driving desire to be close to that blue-eyed beauty staying down there at that ranch.

Cutter pulled the reins and turned the pinto back around for town. A little drinking and gambling would always get his thinking juices flowing. He licked his dry lips and urged the mount into a canter, picturing a big mug of brew in his hand and a black-haired gal on his lap.

Joseph closed his eyes and released a deep sigh. Why in the world did he even try? There was no way he would ever understand these women or any women, for that matter.

"Lydia, I will explain everything to Joseph ..." Emily's words halted when Lydia shook her head.

"Thank you, Emily, but that's not necessary," Lydia spoke just above a whisper and turned wide eyes toward Joseph. "I would rather tell Joseph myself."

Emily patted the young woman's hand and turned sympathetic eyes to her son. "Of course, dear, I understand. Joseph, why don't you take Lydia to the patio while I help clear the table?"

Well, Joseph had made a big mistake, and now he was going to have to pay for it. Looking at his mother told him she was dead serious about this and dared him to raise an objection. The muscles in his neck tightened, and his jaw clenched just thinking about being alone in the garden with a woman that needed consoling!

With one more look toward his mother, he pushed his chair back and forced himself to attend to Lydia's chair as he had been taught. He lightly touched her elbow and guided her to the door that led out to the patio.

There had been days when he was younger that he had day-dreamed of taking a beautiful woman to the patio garden in the dusky evening. He would have led her to an intimate corner and motioned for her to sit beside him on the tiny iron bench, quite sure that they would have to snuggle due to its small size. Then he would have slipped a long arm around the back of the bench and gazed at his lady in the moonlight.

But that was a dream! He had to keep his wits about him, and remember, no matter what, that he could not fall in love with Lydia Silverstreet!

He held the door for her as she passed through and into the patio. The bright moonlight cast a romantic air about the garden. Joseph swallowed hard and ran a finger around his collar, thinking how warm it was this evening. Before he gave it a thought, he had taken Lydia's slim hand and placed it securely in the crook of his arm.

Great! Banister, what are you doing? You are supposed to run from this woman not hold on to her! Joseph warned himself, but his thoughts wavered, and he tried to justify himself. *Oh well, it's too late now. I can't just move her hand since I'm the one that put it there. After all, I'm just behaving as a gentleman should!*

Lydia breathed, "This is such an enchanted garden."

They began to stroll around the patio looking at the various garden plots, though never seeing anything but each other.

"Mother had quite a fight with my father over this garden patio," Joseph informed her, enjoying the way she felt at his side. "You see, Father drew up the plans for the wing with the bedrooms to come out from the middle of the front section, like a giant *T*."

He stopped and turned them so they faced the main section of the house. Then he leaned down and in closer to point it out to her. He inhaled deeply of her sweet-smelling hair.

"But Mother kept after him about moving the bedroom wing over to the edge of the front section so she could have her patio." He moved his arm toward the far corner of the house.

Joseph watched as Lydia's eyes followed his arm, and then she turned and smiled at him. Their faces were so close. Their eyes held each other's for long moments, and when she spoke, it sounded breathless, "I see your mother had her way." A smile tugged at her mouth, and her eyes twinkled.

Joseph's wild heartbeat snapped him into attention. His grin was lopsided as his free hand moved to massage the suddenly very tense muscles in his neck. *What am I doing?* he asked himself. He willed his feet to move and prayed she couldn't hear how hard his heart was beating.

After several moments, he began again, "Father finally conceded and built the bedroom wing the way Mother wanted it, but she waited several more years before she had her garden patio. In fact, it wasn't until Father was sick and couldn't fight her over it any longer."

"It is so beautiful. I've never seen anything like it."

"Mother had an idea of what she wanted, but it really took shape with the help of Carlos and Maria. They gave it a sort of courtyard look."

Joseph and Lydia had slowly rambled around the garden several times. When a silence fell between them, they were standing in front of a bench in the most secluded part of the garden. Now what should he do?

Run! Run for your life, Joseph Banister! You don't want to be here with her. It's dangerous!

"Joseph, I would like to tell you about my parents," she reminded him and dropped her eyes to the small bench.

He stalled, "Lydia, I ... I ... um ... there is no need to share this if it is too painful. I know I'm a perfect stranger, and well ... it's none of my business. Besides, I'm sure you're very tired."

Joseph stumbled through what he hoped was a logical reason to drop the subject and leave the garden. He was not prepared for the answer she gave him.

"Joseph," she answered almost bashfully, never realizing the havoc she wreaked on his heart, "I believe that if we are to be—married ..."

There she did it again. When she tilts her head and blushes like that, a tingle runs right through me. I don't know what that means, but it sure does seem hot this evening! Again, he took a finger and ran it around his collar.

Lydia swallowed and started again, "I believe if we are to marry that as husband and wife we should share things together." Taking a deep breath, she plunged in to explain further, "I don't think there should be any secrets between us. My parents had a wonderful friendship as well as a beautiful marriage and ... and that's what I want for us."

Why did she have to bring that up? The girl of my dreams would feel the same way. Whoa there, fella, he warned himself, *don't start comparing her to your dream girl. Remember this is a* nightmare!

Joseph decided to sidestep the marriage talk and head for safer ground. "All right, Lydia, if that's what you want. I ... uh ... I mean ...," he motioned for her to take a seat on the bench.

When he joined her, it was just as he thought it would be. She snuggled up beside him, causing his pulse to speed up at a gallop. He was quite sure she could feel the hard beat of his heart through his shirt, yet she seemed to be completely unaware of the heat that radiated between their touching arms.

Joseph stretched his neck and longed for a cool breeze when he noticed a shiver pass through Lydia's slight frame. Naturally he moved his arm around her shivering shoulders and asked, "Are you cold?"

"Just a little, but I'll be all right now," she assured, smiling up into his eyes.

Joseph needed a distraction desperately, so he began the conversation, "You wanted to tell me about your parents."

Lydia's body tensed, and she looked across the patio at some unknown spot for long moments. When she began her story, the words came out a bit strained. She turned her face toward him, and tears glistened in her eyes.

Oh no, not tears! Joseph groaned to himself. *Lord, I promise you that if she should start to cry, I am done for! I have no resolve left when I see a woman crying. Please, please* help!

Joseph gently took her hand in his and stroked the back of it with his thumb. It was the wrong thing to do, but it felt so natural to try to comfort her. He was rewarded with a weak smile, and her story spilled from her lips. She told him of the love she had for her parents and about the fire that took their lives. Her lip quivered as her gaze met his sympathetic eyes, and she shared the conversation with her aunt Edith. Once again, she confessed her belief that her parents left this world one moment and were in the presence of the Lord Jesus the next.

She stopped and stared deep into his eyes. "Joseph, do you know that if you died right now, you would go to heaven?"

His arm squeezed her shoulders lightly, and he nodded, "Yes, I know that I have accepted the free gift of salvation and received everlasting life."

A beautiful smile spread across her face, and Joseph felt it all the way to his toes. But it was the yawn that escaped her lips that brought the late hour to their attention.

"I'm sorry, Lydia. I have kept you up far too late. I'm sure that your trip was exhausting."

Joseph stood and stretched out his hand for hers. He guided her to the door that led to the bedrooms, walked up the hallway, and stopped at her door. She touched the doorknob to go inside when his words stopped her.

"Lydia," he whispered his voice husky.

The attraction between them had been immediate, and knowing that they had been brought together to marry seemed to add to the magnetism. He found her irresistible.

She turned around, and their eyes locked. He bent low but came to his senses just before his lips dipped to claim hers. He stepped back and mumbled, "The nights are cold here, so stay under the covers." Then he spun around and almost ran for the end of the hall and the safety of his bedroom.

7

THE SCREAM BROKE THE SILENCE of the night, and Joseph sat straight up in his bed. He had been having the same nightmare about his father, but he didn't think he had screamed. As he began to waken, he realized it had been a female scream.

Mother. It was his first thought, and he grabbed up his pants and flew through the door. His chest tightened when he reached her room: the door open and the room empty. Voices from the guest room urged him back into the hallway.

He heard his mother's voice soft and hushed, trying to calm Lydia. He stood just out of sight and listened as Lydia apologized to his mother. His hands trembled as he heard her tell of the dream that had plagued her since her parents' death. The flames, the smoke, and the cries had all been so real to her this time.

Lydia's questions broke his heart. Why? Why had the Lord taken her parents from her? Why did He leave her all alone? How could He have left her with an unbelieving aunt that belittled and berated her for the love she had for Him?

Lydia sobbed out all she had carried as she was held in Emily's motherly embrace. She told of the way her aunt forbid her to attend church and have any fellowship with other believers. Then when her aunt found out that there was no inheritance, she tried to marry Lydia off to a St. Louis socialite.

Listening in the hallway outside Lydia's door, Joseph paced unable to believe all that she had been through. He wanted to rush into the room and let her know that it was all behind her. She would be free to love the Lord and serve Him right here at the Circle B, but he stayed out of sight and prayed that his mother would be able to help her.

Joseph chanced a glimpse into the room and witnessed the tenderness of his mother. He was glad Lydia could experience the love of a mother again yet wondered at the stirrings of his own heart. This woman had only been here for a day, and already she had come to mean something special to both Banisters.

Inside the room, Lydia fell silent as her tears stopped; her breathing was shuddered with a hiccup sporadically escaping her lips. Emily sat on the bed and held Lydia in her arms much like a mother would hold a small child. She rocked back and forth, humming, wiping away her own tears. Then Emily tenderly brushed strands of black hair from Lydia's tear-dampened face.

Her heart broke for this sweet child, and she hoped with all her heart that Joseph would learn to love her. She was such a mix of courage and vulnerability, of love and fear, of confidence and doubt, and she deserved love and happiness, just as her Joseph did.

Emily took several minutes to assure Lydia of her love and support. She had a word of prayer for her and tucked her into the covers, kissing her a good night. Then she moved into the hallway to find Joseph pacing.

"Is she all right?" he asked, concern evident on his face.

"Yes, I think she'll be fine. Oh, Joseph, she has been through so much," she whispered, tears threatening to fall again.

Joseph nodded his agreement, "I know, I heard everything." He reached an arm around his mother and guided her into her room.

"Joseph, we need to talk in the morning."

"Yes, Mother, I know that too. But for now try to sleep," he suggested, tenderly leading her to the edge of her bed. Then he leaned over and whispered, "I love you, Mother." He placed a kiss in her hair and disappeared.

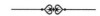

Joseph woke before dawn and dressed, determined to spend some time at the rock. He needed to get some things in perspective and knew being at the rock would help him. He quietly opened his door and tiptoed to the patio, carrying his boots so they wouldn't wake his mother.

As he began to cross the dark patio, a voice startled him so that he almost dropped his boots.

"Joseph, where are you going? I thought you understood we needed to talk this morning?" Emily spoke with pointed disapproval.

Joseph turned toward the voice and squinted his eyes to adjust them to the dusky darkness. In the corner created by the walls, his mother sat at the small wrought iron table.

He padded across the tile floor in his stocking feet, looking much like he had been caught with his hand in the cookie jar. He pulled out a chair for himself and sat across from his mother.

As he worked on slipping into his boots, he questioned, "Were you having trouble sleeping too?"

"Yes, it was a very long night. It took me quite a while to fall into a restless sleep, just to awaken again a few hours later."

"I did some tossing and turning myself," he confessed, pushing his Stetson back and scratching his forehead. "I thought a good ride and some time at the rock would help me this morning." A thick shock of sandy brown hair fell toward his brow, and he brushed it up with his hand and replaced the hat.

"Your father's hair did the same thing," she reminisced.

Joseph stiffened at the reminder of his father. He did not want to be or do anything like him.

Emily's soft laugh turned Joseph's head toward her. "I threatened him many times that I would shave him bald. He would just laugh back and answer, 'Only if you would love a bald man!'"

Silence filled the patio as mother and son drifted into a world of their own thoughts. Then Emily questioned, "Joseph, have I made a terrible mistake?"

The uncertainty in his mother's question startled him. He knew her to be one of the strongest women he'd ever known, always possessing a confidence that had carried her through the hardest of times.

"Is this about Lydia?"

"And you, Joseph."

Joseph released a great sigh. How could he tell his mother that everything was going to be all right when he knew what he had planned for Lydia? If they married, she would be locked into a marriage in name only with no hope of intimacy or children. Just the thought of it made Joseph's shoulders slump in defeat.

"Oh, Joseph, I just want you to be happy, to know true love, and somehow, I believe the Lord will arrange that between you and Lydia." Emily raised her hand to silence Joseph's comment. "I know I've overstepped my boundaries as a mother. I know that in 1900, there should be no arranged marriages, but I also know that the Lord can intervene in our lives to bring about wonderful things."

"I'm sure He can, Mother," he replied, knowing the Lord could but hoping that He would not.

"But ..."

"But ... nothing," he lied.

"You heard last night that she has nothing to go back to. Oh, I imagine her aunt would arrange a marriage," she gave a faint laugh, "about like I have, I guess. But it would be one in name only. There would be no love or happiness for her." Emily paused to wipe a tear from her cheek. "I just couldn't imagine that for Lydia."

Guilt squeezed Joseph's heart, knowing that if Lydia married him that was the deal she would get from their marriage. *But that is all I can offer. There is no way that I can allow myself to love Lydia. There is no way I can allow a child to be born of our union that would carry on this family curse. I must find a way to have that kind of marriage to ensure mother's happiness. After all she has been through, mother deserves that much.* Joseph's thoughts helped him to justify his next statement.

"I will marry Lydia."

"Oh, Joseph, you've made me so happy," she acknowledged with relief. She came around the table and gave her son a warm hug, promising, "I know everything will work out. Just wait and see."

He kissed his mother's cheek and stood to leave.

"Now wait just a minute, Mister," she insisted, "where do you think you're going?" She stood with her hands resting on her slim hips.

Joseph thought it was good to see her back to normal. She was confident that she had control of the situation and she let you know it.

"I'm headed to the rock for little while, remember?" he teased.

"Oh, yes, now I remember," she laughed. "Well, you do *remember* that today is Sunday. There will not be a church service because Preacher Henley had to travel to Raton for his brother's funeral. Go and take care of whatever you have to take care of, but promise me that you will be back for lunch, I have something special planned."

A mischievous twinkle lit her eyes, and Joseph felt a certain trepidation over the noon meal that awaited him, causing an annoying tick in his jaw and a tightening in his neck muscles. Well, he needed to kick his plan into action, and it seemed this afternoon was as good a time as any.

After a short ride, Joseph tethered Titus to a bush and retreated to the rock. He situated himself and peered out over the countryside, vast with its rolling hills and prairie grass. In the distance, he could see a hazy outline that would soon reveal the mountain range. He took a deep breath and exhaled slowly, causing his tense muscles to relax. He loved it here on this rock. He felt as if he could leave his problems behind him and never have another worry in the world.

But in reality, Joseph knew things would never be like that. It seemed that with each new day, there was a new problem to go along with it. Sometimes he felt as if he would be crushed under the weight of them.

He stretched his tall frame out over the rock and allowed the morning sun to warm him. He pushed his hat back high on his head and rubbed his forehead, mulling over the impossible situation his mother had created.

He tried to think it through logically. Most important was the fact that he loved his mother.

You could love Lydia too. The truth passed across his mind.

"I could," he spoke aloud but was unable to put into words his growing feelings for Lydia.

Then it hit him. It was because of his feelings for both women that he must follow through with his plan. For his mother, because he loved her more than life itself. Because he longed to assure that the rest of her days would be filled with happiness. Because she had suffered with a husband that was cruel and heartless. And for Lydia, because she had nothing to go back to. Because she had suffered much at the hand of her aunt. Because at the Circle B, she would be among Christians and able to serve the Lord freely.

You see, I can't possibly have feelings for her. We just met yesterday, Joseph reminded himself. *I don't know much about her. Why, we are just about strangers! Besides, I don't believe in love at first sight!*

When Joseph left the rock, he checked in with Buck and the herd. Everything was going smoothly, and Joseph knew he didn't need to stay around. Buck Hanson was an asset to the ranch. He handled his responsibilities without having to be constantly reminded, and the men respected his abilities to work with man and beast.

Joseph had heard several other neighboring ranchers complaining about their foremen, but he proudly bragged on Buck. Although Buck was older than Joseph, he never tried to use his age to lord over Joseph. Buck showed him the respect due a boss, and in return, Joseph respected him and gave him high praise for his accomplishments.

Joseph's mind traveled back to a conversation he had with Buck about a year after taking the reins of the Circle B. He had to make a hard decision and was second-guessing himself when Buck came along to encourage him. Buck had been hired by Richard Banister, Joseph's father, and had worked his way up to ranch foreman. Buck told him how much he appreciated the changes Joseph had made on the ranch especially in the way he dealt with the men. Buck said that he figured the Lord was pleased with the way Joseph treated each man fairly. That he expected a good day's work and paid a man a fair wage for it. That he demanded the men behave themselves decently and be law-abiding. Buck also thanked Joseph for witnessing to him about the Lord all those years ago. He said that just recently he was able to lead his brother Cody to the Lord.

Joseph wiped his hand down his face, thinking of the things that Buck had not said. Buck had not mentioned the cruel ways his father treated a man or woman as if they were property. He was liberal with his sarcasm and too conservative with his praise. He could have told Buck that he had determined as a young teenager he would not be like his father. In many ways, Joseph acted opposite of his father.

He shook off his thoughts and brought himself back to the work at hand. Monday morning, bright and early, the men would begin spring branding. Joseph growled within himself when he thought about the plans that were in store for him on Monday night. He would rather wrestle a bawling calf in the dirt than face a preacher at the altar!

Nevertheless, his path had been chosen for him, and for his mother's sake, he would follow through. Joseph's stomach grumbled, reminding him he had skipped breakfast. He turned Titus toward home, even though he felt his mother was cooking up something for lunch!

Lydia woke to the smell of coffee lingering in the air. She stretched stiff muscles and bit her lip, hesitant to face Emily after the nightmare last night. It had been so real that she screamed out with fear. She hated the fact that she had wakened Emily, yet it felt so good to be held in a mother's arms, even if they weren't the arms of her own mother.

She hoped that Joseph had not been disturbed but wondered if he could sleep through all the noise. Lydia sat up in her bed and began to undo the long braid of black hair. A smile tugged at her mouth as she pictured Joseph. He really was better looking than she had hoped. Every one of his features testified to the fact he was all man, not like some of the less masculine callers that Aunt Edith had forced upon her.

She estimated him at six feet something, with muscles bulging like she had never seen before. Her face blushed at the thought of the firmness of his chest when she had backed into him on the patio. He was strong, and she felt he would keep her safe.

She gingerly climbed out of the bed and began to brush the long tresses of her hair, remembering Joseph's hair was so thick and a wonderful sandy brown color. She had watched that shock of hair fall across his brow several times and longed to comb it into place with her fingers.

She laid her brush down and looked at her puffy eyes in the mirror. Her lips formed a pout, and she hoped the puffiness would disappear before she saw Joseph. Then she pictured his eyes as they stared into her own outside her door last night. They were so dark brown that they looked black. She knew if the light had been right, she could have seen her reflection in them.

She was so sure he was going to kiss her last night and even this morning just the thought brought a tickle of excitement. She went to the wardrobe and pulled out her pink gingham dress. She hugged it close to her chest and marveled that she could feel this way over a man she had just met.

A knock at her door put a halt to her daydreaming, and Emily's call for breakfast reminded her she was hungry.

She passed through the lovely patio on her way to the dining room and enjoyed remembering how tender Joseph had been the night before. He seemed to like her, and she hoped that today they would have some more time to get to know each other.

During breakfast, Emily explained that Joseph had some chores to tend to but would be back at lunchtime. This allowed the women time to talk about him without interruption. Emily was pleased to hear that Lydia liked him and looked forward to more time with him, but it was the sparkle of her eyes and the blush that encouraged Emily more than Lydia's words.

Nothing was mentioned about the night before, and Emily felt that in time Lydia would feel free to talk to her about it. Instead, she used the morning to show Lydia through the house, hoping to make it feel more like a home to the young woman.

Just off the dining room, they peeked into Joseph's office. Emily showed her the door to the outside and explained that the men used that door instead of having to track through the house. Beside the dining room was a spacious kitchen, with a huge cookstove and a well pump.

Back through the dining room was a large living room with a mammoth rock fireplace on the outside wall. Leather furniture and long horns hanging over the mantel spoke of the masculinity of the room, but it was a door on the other side of the living room that caught Lydia's eye.

Emily smiled and told her of the unfinished upstairs and the hopes that one day it would be filled with hollering little ones. Lydia blushed at the thought, while she confessed that she longed for it just as much as Emily!

The rest of the morning Emily used to find out what kind of belongings Lydia brought with her and of what she might have need. It was decided that they would take a trip to town in the morning to make some necessary purchases before the wedding.

8

JOSEPH SAUNTERED TOWARD THE HOUSE with his hands shoved in his pockets, but when he saw his mother outside the kitchen door, he hurried his pace to speak to her before she entered the kitchen.

"I'm starved," he growled, but the smile on his face reflected his playful mood. "Now, Mother, are you going to tell me what you have been cooking up?" He dropped a kiss on her cheek and leaned against the buggy his mother had been loading.

"No, not yet. I want to tell you and Lydia together."

Joseph's mood changed immediately. He looked around and touched his mother's elbow. "I need to speak with you alone. It's about tomorrow."

Emily's eyes grew wide, and she followed Joseph toward the clothesline, putting some distance between them and the house before she spoke, "What's wrong, Joseph?"

"Well, I have just one request about the ... ceremony tomorrow," he stumbled, too nervous to say the word *wedding*.

Relief was evident on her face, and she nodded for him to continue.

"Since the circumstances are a little out-of-the-ordinary, I hope that you will honor my wishes and make this a very quiet affair. There is no need for guests or even refreshments. I want everything kept low-keyed."

"I understand, but do you think this is fair to Lydia?" she questioned, clearly annoyed.

Of course, it's not fair to Lydia, none of this confounded plan is fair to her. But the hand that is being dealt to me isn't fair either.

Joseph didn't speak his mind but said, "I'm sure it is not fair to Lydia, but nevertheless, that is the way I want it. Promise me you will honor my wishes."

Joseph hated to be so stern with his mother, yet at the same time, he knew her tendency to surprise. This was not a wedding to be celebrated; it was just an agreement between two people to live together. At least, that was to be his understanding.

"All right, son, but I hope you won't regret it. Remember every woman wants to have memories of her special day," she retorted and walked to the kitchen.

Joseph thought that tomorrow's events would never be special to him or Lydia. He pushed his hat back off his forehead and wiped his brow with his sleeve. He left the hat sitting back on his head, shoved his hands in his pockets, and tramped to the house.

He went to the living room and pulled his hot boots off and propped his feet up on the low table in front of him. He leaned back against the leather couch, locking his fingers behind his head. His Stetson was pushed forward over his closed eyes, and he hoped to drift into a peaceful nap.

When Lydia thought that she heard Joseph's voice, she smiled to herself and set her Bible on the nightstand. Anticipation tingled through her; she hoped Joseph noticed her pink dress. It was one of her favorites, believing it made her complexion rosier. She checked on her hair and swept up some stubborn strands that refused to stay in the chignon she had tediously worked on.

She walked up the hallway and entered the living room to find Joseph stretched out comfortably on the couch. It was hard to believe that she was so drawn to him this soon.

She silently moved behind the couch and bent close to his ear.

"Well now, that looks mighty comfortable," Lydia whispered.

Joseph jumped, knocking his hat to the floor and smacking Lydia in the face with his long arm. The distinct sound of skin meeting skin echoed through the room as he turned to see what he hit. Lydia stood stunned holding her cheek. Tears glistened in her wide eyes, and she was unable to hide the look of fear that covered her face.

"Oh, Lydia," he mumbled and vaulted over the couch to check on her cheek. But when he took a step toward her, she backed away like a wounded animal.

"Please forgive me. I had no idea you were behind me," he apologized, reaching his hand out to touch her arm.

She stood very still and allowed Joseph to move her hand so he could examine her red cheek. His fingertips moved gently over her soft, creamy skin. He checked to be sure nothing was broken. Then without a warning, he glanced a soft kiss on her swelling cheek.

She closed her eyes with the sweetness of his touch, and two small tears slid down her face. His fingertips tenderly swept them away, and she met his gaze with dreamy, blue eyes.

Suddenly, he stepped back as if he had been the one smacked. She reached out to grab him, but he sidestepped her arm and moved into the hallway and down to his room.

A single tear slid down Lydia's swollen cheek. "He didn't even notice my pink dress," she fretted.

A little later when the word came that it was time for lunch, Lydia dreaded facing Emily with a red swollen cheek, but she had no choice. Emily's eyes widen with question when she saw Lydia, but she never asked. She was not given an explanation for Lydia's cheek or Joseph's foul mood; however, Joseph assured his mother everything was all right. Lydia's silence screamed otherwise.

When Emily announced her plans had changed, Joseph insisted upon knowing what they had been. It seemed that Joseph could charm anything out of his mother, and she spilled the beans on the surprise picnic for two.

Lydia was in no mood for a picnic, especially if it meant being alone with Joseph. She wanted time to figure this man out, and she felt she could do that better alone. But when Joseph learned of the trouble Emily had gone through to prepare things, he loaded a wary Lydia into the buggy and headed for a shady spot along the riverside.

Neither Joseph nor Lydia spoke a word as they rode the bumpy path to the river. The scenery became a lush green the closer they got to the water, and along the riverbank were some shade trees. The buggy stopped just under the trees, and Joseph came around to help Lydia out. When she refused to take his hand, he pleaded with her, and she stepped from the buggy.

Joseph spread a quilt out under a tree and carried the basket of food over. Lydia stood with her arms wrapped around her midsection watching him move about as if nothing had happened back at the house. She wasn't blaming him for hitting her in the cheek because she knew it had been an accident, but she didn't understand why he withdrew from her every time it seemed he had been attracted to her. After all that *was* a good thing: to be attracted to the woman you were to marry.

Lydia concluded that Joseph was not pleased with her. There was only one thing to do—return to St. Louis. Perhaps it was for the best, before she became too attached to these people and this place.

Joseph had swiftly laid out the lunch and motioned for her to join him. She moved stiffly to the quilt and sat down opposite him.

"Joseph," Lydia broke the silence, "I want you to take me to get the train first thing in the morning."

Joseph's jaw dropped, and he stared at her with unbelief.

Lydia spoke again before Joseph could reply, "I guess, I am just not what you were expecting. I'm sorry I displease you so." Her last few words were said just above a whisper. She bowed her head and hated herself for crying. It was all too much: losing her parents, living with Aunt Edith, and coming to New Mexico.

At the sight of her tears, Joseph was at her side. He took a finger and raised her chin so he could look into her eyes as he spoke, "Lydia, I'm sorry about hitting your cheek." Tenderly, he caressed her wounded cheek.

His touch made her skin tingle and her pulse race. Her eyes closed in delight until she remembered that he misunderstood. She shook her head and opened her mouth to explain, but Joseph placed his fingertips on her lips to stop her words.

"I would never have knowingly hit you, Lydia. Please believe me. I don't think a man should touch a woman like that," he tried to explain. "It upset me to see your tears and think that you believed I would hit you."

She took her small hand, smoothed his furrowed brow, and stroked his eyebrows and nose. Her fingers caressed his cheeks and traced over his top lip and then the bottom. She longed to show him she forgave him but settled with just telling him.

Joseph let out a huge sigh and grabbed her in a bone-crushing bear hug.

"Lydia, tell me you'll stay and marry me," he implored.

Lydia could hardly breathe. How did he expect her to answer him! She felt the pounding of his heart pulse through her and felt sure he was sincere.

"Yes! You're crushing me!" she squeaked out, praying he could hear her.

"Good," he released his bear hug and pushed her away. "I'm starved, let's eat."

A shocked Lydia stared in amazement as Joseph jumped back to his place and offered a quick prayer over the food. She had just been passed over for roast beef! Her eyes were wide with unbelief that he had just proposed, then threw her away! It was as if he were relieved to have it done and over with.

Squinting one eye and tilting her head to one side, she tried to figure out what exactly had just happened. Shouldn't she be ecstatic over the proposal? Shouldn't she be filled with rapture and bubbling over with excitement? Shouldn't Joseph have swept her into his arms and smothered her with kisses full of love and promise?

Then why did she feel so let down? So discarded? *Oh, Lord, have I jumped ahead of you and made a terrible mistake?* Doubt filled her and threatened to choke her.

The rest of the picnic had been a blur to Lydia. She keenly felt the disappointment of the proposal and was astonished at how much Joseph changed when they arrived home and met his mother.

He hugged on Lydia and sent her looks of love, but only when they were with his mother. He proudly told his mother that he had proposed to Lydia, and she had gladly accepted his proposal. He dropped a whisper of a kiss on Lydia's cheek as a reward for her acceptance and pulled his mother into a tender embrace.

Lydia almost felt jealous of the way Joseph gently held his mother for long moments and whispered things into her ear. Emily responded with giddy laughter, then left his arms to hug Lydia.

Lydia knew Emily was sincere, but she was beginning to wonder what kind of a game Joseph was playing. Perhaps it was just her imagination that he was treating her coolly, while his mother received his warmth.

Lydia massaged tight temples and stretched her aching back, hoping to dispel such dark thoughts. She felt she would be sick if she had to stand there much longer and watch the way Joseph was behaving. She excused herself, and Emily said she understood, after all it wasn't every day that a woman becomes engaged!

Joseph had excused himself quickly after Lydia left the room. He hated himself for the way he had treated her and knew she was miserable. He could hardly believe she had suggested going back to St. Louis. His mother would have been so brokenhearted. He had to resort to drastic measures for the sake of his plan. But it cost him dearly to persuade her to stay.

She tempted him to forsake his plan, to forget the curse, and to love her without reservation. He came so close to kissing her after smacking her in the cheek that he just had to run away. He couldn't tell her that for the first time he doubted he would be able to keep her at arm's length.

Joseph took a steadying breath and reminded himself, *Easy does it, Joseph. Remember this is just part of the plan. Don't get let your feelings get out of control. You don't love this little woman. You just feel sorry for her!*

But there was no denying the flip-flops his heart did when she said she would marry him.

While the two young people wrestled with their feelings, Emily was beside herself with joy. Instead of the engaged couple spilling over with happiness, it was Emily that floated through the house. Finally her Joseph would know true love and happiness. And sweet Lydia, whom she had already come to love as a daughter, would make Joseph a wonderful bride!

She made arrangements to have an engagement dinner in the garden that night. Every candle and candelabra in the house was placed in the garden, bathing the patio in romantic candlelight.

Emily was so excited about the wedding that she never noticed the strain between the newly engaged couple. She carried the conversation much to their relief, and Lydia couldn't help but listen with interest as Emily told the story of how the Banisters came to be in the New Mexico Territory.

"You know, Lydia," Emily began, "the Banisters were originally from St. Louis too. I guess that is why I used the St. Louis newspapers." She smiled warmly at Lydia, thanking the Lord for answering her prayers once again.

She continued, "It was Joseph's great-grandfather Banister that first had the idea to move west. It was in 1830 that he and Joseph's grandfather met Jedediah Smith. Have you heard of him?"

"No, I don't think so," Lydia replied.

"Well, he was a famous mountain man in those days. He trapped and explored a good part of the West. For eight years, Jed Smith roamed the western United States trapping beaver."

Joseph laughed and put in, "It's said that when he was twenty-six years old, he trapped 668 pelts in one season!" Joseph shook his head, clearly delighted with the story.

Emily continued, "Yes, he was quite a man. He traveled to California and up to Oregon. Why, he led the expedition that discovered the South Pass that opened up a wagon trail into Oregon!

"He was an unusual sort of mountain man though, because he was a Christian. The story goes that he used to ride the trails singing Methodist hymns. He was clean-shaven too, unlike most mountain men with big bushy beards. He kept a fine testimony by avoiding whiskey and women. Friends of Jed's said that he was 'a bold, outspoken, and consistent Christian.' His Bible and his rifle were the two friends that he always carried with him. But his men didn't know what to think of Jed. They said that he was 'half grizzly and half preacher.' He earned the name 'Knight in Buckskin' because of his adventures.

"Well, let's get back to the Banisters. You see, Jed Smith retired to St. Louis in 1830, and that is where great-grandfather Banister met him. He was so impressed by the mountain man and the things he said about the West that great-grandfather Banister determined to move his family."

"Granny Banister used to say that's when Gramps caught the wanderlust bug," Joseph added.

"Yep, from that day on, he saved every cent he could in hopes of one day moving out West," finished Emily.

"So it was your great-grandfather that settled the Circle B?" Lydia inquired.

"No," Joseph took up the story. "He lost a little of his excitement when he heard that Jed Smith had left St. Louis to lead a wagon train to Santa Fe and had been killed by a band of Comanche.

"But it was my grandfather, who had also met Jed Smith at just eight years old, that added to his father's savings and moved his family to the wild territories. My father, Richard, was grown and married when they moved to start the Circle B. Over the years, we were able to buy out neighboring ranches to make the ranch what it is today." He smiled with pride.

9

DIRK CUTTER LOVED DARKNESS. HE wasn't sure if it was because most of his dastardly deeds were committed under the cover of darkness or because he hated the light. He knew that in the light, every evil work could be seen.

The Sunday night moon shone brightly and guided Cutter right to the Circle B herd that had been gathered for branding. The long horns milled around uneasy for this time of the night, which would only help with Cutter's scheme. Just as he had figured, there were only two cowpokes watching over the herd, while the rest of them were bedded down for the night.

A sly grin crossed Cutter's face; this was almost too easy. He found a small rise to hide behind and spotted the two men riding the night watch. He quietly observed them for several hours until one of the men left his horse and walked to a nearby bush.

Cutter moved stealthily through the weeds until he was beside the cowboy's horse. He carefully grabbed the cinch strap and slashed it almost in half. He silently backed into the shadows just before the cowboy stepped back to his horse.

As the cowboy mounted the horse, one foot in the stirrup and the other in midair, the cinch snapped in half throwing the cowboy to the ground with a loud thud. As he hit the hard, dry ground, the bone in his arm snapped in two, causing a painful howl to escape his lips. It was just enough to spook the already restless beeves to stampede.

Cutter watched the injured cowboy barely miss being trampled by the angry herd by pulling himself onto a nearby rock. The raging herd of long horns thundered past him creating a thick cloud of dust. It was a successful night.

Joseph fretted and squirmed, of all mornings for his mother to insist he stay for breakfast. He knew she was trying to get the day, his wedding day, started off right, but he wanted to be out on the range. Today was branding day, and Joseph needed to be with his men, but instead he sat on the patio sipping coffee and making small talk.

The day promised to be a warm one, and already perspiration gathered around his collar.

Maybe Lydia's lovely presence is causing my temperature to rise.

Joseph's thoughts made him growl out loud. The women turned to see what was wrong with him as Juan rushed into the garden and told Joseph a rider was coming in "really hard." That usually meant trouble, and Joseph jumped to his feet and set his hat in place. His mother mumbled under her breath, and Joseph hesitated for just a few moments. He knew she was disappointed by the interruption, but it was his salvation.

Buck appeared at the side gate, and Joseph went to meet him, a sickening feeling gnawing his insides. Since Buck looked tired and upset, Joseph tried to keep his temper in check. Buck apologized from the beginning, and Joseph knew that meant something was really wrong. Buck told him that Rusty Callahan had fallen getting into his saddle because his cinch strap had been cut. The fall caused his arm to break exposing the bone. When he hollered in pain, the restless cattle began to stampede. It took the men the rest of the night to get the herd under control and calmed down. Rusty was with Red, the camp cook, but he would probably need to go into town to see the doc. Buck explained that he had talked to Rusty, and the man couldn't be sure, but he thought that he had heard a gunshot right before the stampede. Buck had gone out to the range in hopes of finding some signs that would help him understand what had happened, but the evidence had been covered by the dust the herd had stirred up.

Joseph let out a loud "Doggone" and snapped his Stetson off his head smacking it to his leg. Frustration filled Joseph, and he began to pace. Someone had hurt a cowboy and started a stampede deliberately. The territory had had its share of range wars, like the Lincoln County wars and several small range wars time and again, but so far the Circle B had been fortunate to stay clear of any trouble.

He glanced back at his mother and Lydia. It was a bad day to have a scattered herd and a dog-tired bunch of cowboys. He knew that this meant rounding up the scattered beeves and delaying the branding. There was no way of getting around several more long days in the saddle until things were back in order.

He asked Buck if his kid brother, Cody, was available to help, but Buck laughed and reminded Joseph that Cody preferred the rails to the range. The boy loved being an undercover railroad detective. But Buck assured Joseph that there was no need to hire anyone. Buck said it didn't look like there were many stragglers, and with any luck, they would have them rounded up and ready to brand by midweek.

Joseph directed Buck to arrange shifts for the men, allowing some to get a little shut-eye. Before Buck left, Joseph told him to see that Rusty got to Doc Sloan in town and assured him that he would be out on the range shortly.

Joseph watched Buck head back out before he turned to explain to the women. If someone had cut the cinch strap of Rusty's saddle and started the stampede, he wasn't so sure he liked the idea of the women going into town alone. He would arrange for Carlos to escort them.

Not even a stampede could have frustrated the women and their plans for the day. They were going to shop! Emily told Lydia that usually a young woman received household things for wedding gifts, but since Lydia was entering an established household, she planned to work solely on her wardrobe.

It was Christmas in the spring for Lydia. They started in Herzstein's Mercantile and with the ready-to-wear garments. Lydia blushed as Emily chose frilly underclothes along with the usual garments. Then Emily held up two beautiful shirtwaists and lovely skirts. Lydia tried to stop her or at least slow her down, but Emily was on a mission. She was soon to have a daughter-in-law that needed large amounts of spoiling, and she planned to do a good part of it today!

Layer after layer of lovely clothing began to stack up on the counter. Emily was having the time of her life. And Lydia followed the older woman around the store in a daze, wiping tears of joy from her face. Oh, how she had missed having a mother!

The Herzstein's tallied and packaged one thing after another and sent it out to the wagon by Carlos. As they left the mercantile, Lydia was overwhelmed with the quantity of packages in the wagon.

She could hardly believe her eyes when Emily steered her in the directions of Evan's Mercantile on the corner of First and Main. Lydia felt that Emily had everything covered until she saw Emily approach the yard goods. Lydia shook her head, but Emily could not be dissuaded. Yard after beautiful yard was added to their purchases.

When Lydia estimated the purchases, she was horrified, but Emily Banister was radiant. She grabbed up Lydia's arm and insisted they have lunch in the Clayton House dining room. Throughout the meal, the women talked, getting to know each other better.

Lydia was sure that they would head to the full wagon after lunch, but Emily turned and walked a short distance to the dressmakers. Carlos had already delivered the yard goods, and Emily spoke with Mrs. Everly about sewing some new outfits for Lydia. The old seamstress measured every body part that Lydia had and scribbled her measurements in a big book.

They talked about the outfits Mrs. Everly would sew for Lydia and settled on the right cloth for each. Then to Emily's great pleasure, Mrs. Everly produced a beautiful light blue silk gown with a hazy print that had never been picked up. They had Lydia try it on, and with a few nips and tucks, the gown looked as if it had been made for her. Emily watched Lydia look at herself in the full-length mirror. When Lydia looked up and saw Emily watching her, she turned around and gave Emily a hug thanking her over and over again. Emily looked into the young woman's eyes and told her she looked like a princess.

The gown was beautiful with a high neckline filled with a delicate white lace that extended to meet the lightweight silk bodice. The neckline of the bodice was straight across and slightly over the shoulders, which were covered with the same lovely lace as the upper bodice. Dainty lace outlined the silk neckline and a darker blue, silky ribbon created the illusion of dress straps. The bodice fell to the tiny waist in a ballooning fashion with a ribbon belt scalloped with white lace. The skirt fell into three layers, each with scalloped lace edges. The hemline was floor-length and had an extending train.

Lydia's tear-filled eyes met Emily's, and they knew this would become her wedding gown. The beautiful blue brought out the crystal color of her eyes, and Emily knew Joseph would appreciate her beauty.

Mrs. Everly carefully wrapped the gown in paper, and Carlos loaded it into the wagon. The women had enjoyed a prosperous day together and headed home.

Cutter slept in after his long night of havoc. He missed breakfast but treated himself to very large lunch. That was when he saw *her*. She and an older lady were sitting across the hotel dining room enjoying a lunch themselves. Although Cutter was ravenous, he stopped eating and just stared at the blue-eyed beauty. Never had he seen such a beautiful woman.

He had hoped that someone from the Circle B would have contacted him by now, but there was nothing. He would wait a few more days and cause a little more trouble. He had to get on that ranch and be close to that woman. He was sure that he could win her over, but if not, he would just take her!

He sat there watching her until his food got cold. Her smile was contagious, and her laughter floated across the room and delighted his ears. Her silky black hair was pinned up in a loose bun, and she frequently ran her hand up the back of her neck, checking for wayward strands. She moved her hands as she spoke to her companion, and one time, she twirled a strand of hair in her fingertips.

Cutter was stirred just gazing at her from across the room. Determination filled him, or perhaps it was lust, and he knew he would stop at nothing to have her. His conscience told him that following your lusts would cause you to be careless and make dangerous mistakes, but his desire was too great and his ego too large for him to consider failure.

The ladies laughed and shared all the way home. Emily's excitement over the wedding was infectious, and soon Lydia dismissed her earlier apprehensions about Joseph as imagination. She became as giddy as a bride should be on her wedding day. While the women were in town, Maria had moved Lydia's belongings into Joseph's room and Emily's into Lydia's room as Emily had instructed, leaving the guest room between the two occupied rooms. That would give the young couple a bit of privacy.

Unloading the wagon was a chore, and Lydia became unnerved when she realized that she would be putting her new clothes away in Joseph's room. But Emily laughed and told her she had better get used to it!

They grabbed an early light supper and began preparations for the preacher's arrival at eight o'clock. Each of the women bathed, and Emily helped Lydia with her hair. It was decided that Lydia would hide out and dress in her old room, now Emily's. Emily would see to Joseph's dinner and make sure he was cleaned up and dressed for the occasion.

Joseph was dog-tired when he headed for home, but it was a good tired. It had been a long, hard day in the saddle, but a very successful one. Most of the strays had been rounded up with hopes that the job would be finished tomorrow and branding would begin on Wednesday.

Rusty had been to the doctor and had the broken bone set. He would be out of work for several weeks, but Joseph rather liked the idea of having him stay close to the ranch house considering the trouble of the night before. Buck assured him that extra men would stand night watch from now on, and Joseph planned to add to the men's pay for all the extra work they were putting out.

As Joseph arrived home, he had been glad for the day of work; it had been a grateful distraction from his thoughts and the events taking place that evening. He swallowed hard, pushed his Stetson off his forehead, and set his jaw with the determination that his plan would work.

That determination faded when he opened his wardrobe later and saw the frilly, feminine dresses of Lydia hanging next to his clothes.

Oh, Lord, what am I getting into? He sank down on his bed and moaned. A knock at the door reminded him he had to hurry; there was no time to second-guess now. After bathing, Joseph dressed in the clothes that were laid out for him. Black pants, a crisp white shirt, and a ribbon tie stared back at him from his mirror. He raked through his hair and released a breath of pent-up nerves. The tie around his neck felt like a noose he was creating for himself, and he was sure, one way or another, he would be hung by the rope of his own making!

He knew that he would have to talk to Lydia after the ceremony, and he didn't look forward to it. How would she take it? Would she run to his mother with the details of his plan, or would she share in the loyalty that he felt toward his mother?

Joseph glanced at the coat his mother asked him to wear and couldn't bring himself to put it on; instead, he found a black leather vest and shrugged into that. He was tempted to put his Stetson on, but thought better of it.

He walked slowly down the hall and into the living room, feeling much like a condemned man taking his walk to the gallows. His eyes roamed across the room, and he was relieved to see his mother had not made an affair of this thing.

What a night! Preacher Henley was early, Emily was elated, Lydia was giddy, and Joseph was sick! And it was Joseph that set the mood. There was little conversation as the minutes ticked by until eight o'clock.

Joseph wasn't really sure why they waited, but they did, and when the hour rolled around, the preacher stood, and Emily shoved Joseph up beside him. Then she ran down the hallway to get the waiting bride.

Lydia entered the living room with the poise and grace of the princess she looked to be. She was a heavenly sight in her new gown, and his mother glowed with satisfaction. Lydia walked with her eyes locked on Joseph.

His jaw dropped as Lydia floated across the floor toward him. He swallowed hard and ran a nervous finger around his collar. She was more beautiful than he had ever seen her. The gown cast a hazy glow about her, and her eyes held his with a magnetism.

When she smiled, he smiled back. When she stepped beside him, he took her small hand in his large one. When she said "I will," he said, "I will." When she said, "I do," he said, "I do." When she turned toward him with adoring eyes and waiting lips, he balked like a mule!

Wait just a minute, Joseph! You must draw the line. If you taste of her sweet lips, you will have to surrender! Surrender? No way, surrender is not *an option.*

Joseph dropped a quick peck on Lydia's cheek and bounced back to attention. Quiet congratulations were shared, and the preacher begged to be excused after his long trip to Raton.

The three Banisters looked at each other dumbfounded. Emily made the first move by kissing Joseph and wishing him every happiness possible. She hugged Lydia close and shed a few tears before whispering her love and prayers for a long, happy life. Then she discreetly excused herself.

Joseph stood like a fool in the middle of the living room shifting his weight from foot to foot, looking at everything but his new bride.

He had no idea how much his boyish good looks appealed to Lydia. He wished he could bed down with his horse, Titus, but he knew that was impossible.

Lydia moved close beside him and whispered his name, sending chills up his neck. She took his big hand and tugged him ever so gently until she had him moving in the direction of *their* room.

I was mistaken before. This *is what it feels like to head to the gallows!*

She opened the door and had to pull him inside. Joseph watched as she moved closer to him wrapping her small arms around his waist. She gazed up into his eyes, asking for his tender lips to touch hers.

But instead, he grabbed her hands, ripping apart the embrace and pushed them away from him. "Stop it," he hissed, grabbing her slim shoulders and squeezing them tight until tears welled up in her eyes. "Now sit down. It's time you knew the truth."

10

Joseph paced in front of Lydia; he hated the monster he had become. He hated the way he towered over her and made her seem so small and fragile. But what was done was done. He stopped in front of her and raked shaking fingers through his thick hair. He must be hard. He must let her know that there was no hope. He must be sure that she would not jeopardize his mother's happiness. He must make her understand, above all, that this was not a real marriage!

He opened his mouth to speak when he saw it. One small tear that glistened as it slid down her cheek. Joseph groaned.

Ignore the tears, Joseph. Believe me there will be more than one by the time this is over, so you might as well get used to them now!

Joseph took a deep breath and started again, "Lydia, the truth is I never wanted a wife. This was all Mother's idea. I tried to get her to send you back"—he waved his arm—"but she insisted. Once she rolled this thing into motion, I had no way of stopping it."

Lydia sat still with her arms wrapped tight around her waist.

"I want you to understand I'm sorry that you were thrown into the middle of this," Joseph stopped and leaned close to her face, "this farce of a marriage," he sneered.

Lydia gasped in shock.

He stood and turned quickly before she could see how much this was costing him. He walked to the bed and removed a small chunk of wood from the footboard and headboard. Then he removed a long slab of wood from under the bed. He carefully placed it into the notched place in the headboard and into the foot board. It precisely divided the huge bed into two sections.

Lydia watched carefully and looked confused as Joseph stalked back to the couch.

He pointed back to the bed and snapped, "See, this is not a real marriage, and it never will be. I don't love you, Lydia, and I never will."

He expected her to scream or cry or lash out at him. But she sat there like a small child that had been reprimanded by a parent. Joseph winced with the thought that this was how he must have looked when his father had lashed out at him.

He paced around the room sick of himself and this pitiful life he was forced to live. He decided to explain it all to her and hoped that if she knew all his reasons, maybe she wouldn't hate him so much. He pulled a chair over and sat down directly in front of her. He rubbed his chin and massaged his neck muscles.

"Lydia, I grew up with a father and grandfather that were constantly abusive to their wives because of their ill-tempers. They would berate and belittle them to tears. I remember many a night hearing my mother crying long after everyone in the house was supposed to be asleep. Eventually, angry words turned into slaps and bruises." Joseph winced with pain as if he were even then hearing his father hit his mother.

"I hoped that once my grandparents passed away that Father would try to treat Mother better, but it got worse. Lydia, he couldn't help himself, for he was acting just like his father. That's when I realized it had been something passed to him from my grandfather. The men of my family inherited wicked tempers that caused them to hurt the ones they loved in the worst kind of ways."

Lydia laid a hand on Joseph's arm and tried to interrupt, but he shook his head and continued, "Don't you see, even as a young boy I saw it in me." He rasped out the horrible truth. "I knew that it was not right for a man to hurt his wife, and I promised myself I would never marry and treat a wife like my father treated my mother. And I won't pass this on to a son. It's a curse that must stop with me."

He stared at her with despondent brown eyes, his broad shoulders sagging from the weight of his burden.

With a heavy sigh, he went on, "Lydia, I love my mother, and I have devoted my life to make the rest of her life happy. That is why I agreed to go through with this scheme. And I hope you will go along with it too. In Mother's presence, I want her to believe that we are a happily married couple, but when we retire to this room, there will be no ...," he paused unsure of a delicate way to put it.

Another tired sigh departed his lips, and he stood, explaining, "Lydia, I will never exercise my husbandly prerogatives."

They blushed simultaneously and shifted their gaze in other directions. Once again Joseph listened for sobbing or something, but when he turned around, Lydia was very composed.

"Joseph, having a temper—"

"Lydia, I am not going to discuss or debate this with you. This is the way things have to be. Do you understand?" he barked out.

"Yes, Joseph," she meekly replied.

"Now I am going to leave and give you some time to get ready for bed. When you are done, turn the lamp down low," he commanded as he made quick steps to escape the room.

Lydia's tears fell as the door closed behind Joseph. She happened to glance toward the cold fireplace. The smell of ashes assailed her senses and made her gag. She stared at the fireplace; the fire was gone, the hearth cold. It felt like her heart. Just moments ago, the fire in her heart burned with excitement and anticipation, but now it was cold, unfeeling, and dead.

She dropped to her knees beside the small couch and began to pray. She confessed her fear and discouragement over her marriage to Joseph. She begged the Lord for a way out of this pretend marriage, but only peace was whispered to her soul.

As her heart and mind quieted, the Lord helped her to realize that Joseph was a good and honorable man. He had made his decisions because he loved so deeply: his mother and a wife and child he didn't even have at the time.

He was willing to forego his own happiness for the happiness of another.

"He is worth fighting for," she whispered as the Lord renewed her hope. "Lord, with your help, we will help Joseph to know the truth. Please help me to lean on you and not my feelings and to be the kind of wife that would please You. In Jesus name, amen."

She wiped tears from her cheeks and thought about changing her gown. She glanced around the room and remembered the frilly nightgown Emily had purchased for this very night. She would save it with the promise that the Lord would bless them with a real marriage one day.

She took out her plain, cotton nightgown and reached back over her head to unfasten the buttons of her wedding gown. She bit her bottom lip when she pictured the line of delicate buttons on the back of that gown. There was no way she would be able to take care of them herself. Before the wedding, Emily had fastened them for her.

Joseph. She would have to get him back to help her, knowing she could not go and ask Emily. She lowered the lamp and apprehensively awaited his arrival. When he saw that Lydia was still in her gown, his face turned red, and he pointed a shaking finger at her while opening his mouth to speak.

"Joseph," she tried to explain before he lost his temper, "there is no way that I can unbutton my gown."

Joseph's steps were halted halfway into the room, and there he stood frozen to the spot unsure he wanted to be that close to Lydia.

When he made no move toward her, she smiled. "I could go ask your mother ..."

"No," he snapped and jumped forward. Hesitantly he moved behind her and lifted trembling fingers to the first small button. He fumbled with the tiny objects so foreign to his large hands; long moments passed before he was successful and moved on to the next one.

As he wrestled with each new button, his fingers brushed soft, smooth skin. It unnerved him and made each new button a little harder to open, and each time he was successful, the gown opened even more, revealing more skin and starting the circle again.

The sweet scent of her hair drifted up to his nose, and unconsciously he began to deeply inhale the rose scent.

By the time Joseph had unbuttoned the long row, his heart was racing, and great drops of sweat beaded around his forehead. He stepped away from her, wiped his brow with his sleeve, raked shaking fingers through his hair, and headed for the door. He stopped with his hand still on the knob. He'd been out one time; if he left again, someone might become suspicious.

"Lydia," he spoke without looking at her, "I can't go out *again*."

"Well, stay turned around, and I will change quickly," she suggested and teasingly added, "and no peeking!"

He growled in response.

Lydia had stood perfectly still and even smiled to herself, as she felt his shaky fingers struggling to unbutton the gown. A sigh of relief signaled the success of each unfastened button as one by one he moved down the back of her silk gown. She knew very well that the gown sported a whopping twenty-two small, pearl-shaped buttons, tedious even for a woman. She would hold him captive for quite a while.

She hoped that by having Joseph so close, she could persuade him to change his mind, but when she tried to open a conversation, he told her he did not want to talk about it now or ever again. She would pray.

When he finished, he practically ran to the door, before he realized he couldn't leave the room a second time. When she teased him not to peek while she changed her clothes, he crossed his arms over his chest in a huff. The back of his neck turned a bright red with embarrassment. She thought it was the most endearing thing she had ever seen.

When she told him she was finished, he had fully expected to see her safely covered and on her side of the bed. But instead she stood in a white, floor-length nightgown in the middle of the floor. He wasn't sure how much more of this he could handle!

He paced around the room, while she took the pins out of her hair, allowing shiny, black tresses to fall over her shoulders. He stared as she used her fingers to shake lose any tangles. Never had he seen so much hair. Where had she been keeping it? He shoved his hands into his pockets and moved toward the open window longing for a cool breeze.

Lydia retrieved her hair brush from the dresser and began brushing with long, steady strokes. Joseph just stood staring; then, she held out the brush to him, silently asking for his help. His eyes grew wide, and he shook his head quite forcefully. He felt he had helped her enough for one lifetime, and he was quite sure he would not survive through another time.

She took time to carefully plait her black masses into a single, thick braid that she flipped to her back. Finally Lydia got into the bed and covered herself up! Joseph blew the lamp out and slipped out of his clothes and into the other half of the bed. Although the board through the middle of the bed pulled the covers, Joseph was thankful to have it between them.

"Good night, Joseph," Lydia's soft voice broke through the silence of the room.

After all he had told her, she was still as sweet as ever. He just didn't understand it. She had accepted everything he said and obeyed his every wish. He had been sure that he would have to face a ferocious wildcat, scratching and clawing into him, but instead she was an adorable, little kitten waiting to be petted and loved.

He sighed again, thinking that he had been doing a lot of sighing lately and mumbled a good night. Minutes had passed when Joseph felt the bed move ever so slightly and heard Lydia's small voice in prayer.

"Dear Heavenly Father, I thank you for this day and all your blessings. Thank you for providing the beautiful clothes by the thoughtfulness of Emily. Bless her, Lord, in a very special way for all the kindness she has shown me. And thank you for this ranch and the home it affords me. Thank you for Joseph and the hard work he has put into the Circle B.

"Please watch over Rusty and heal his arm quickly. Watch over the ranch, the herd, and the men that help us. Keep them safe and healthy. Watch over Emily and continue to use her to be a blessing to others. Watch over Joseph and give him wisdom and understanding as he oversees the ranch.

"And, Lord, I thank you for our marriage, and I beg you to help me to love my husband and be the wife I am supposed to be before You. In Jesus name, amen."

11

LYDIA SLEPT BETTER THAN SHE had dreamed she would have slept. She peeked over the board and found Joseph gone. Filled with disappointment, she fell back against her pillow and twirling a loose strand of hair, making plans for her Joseph. A smile pulled at the corners of her mouth, and she jumped from the bed with a delicious idea.

She quickly dressed in a new white shirtwaist and a lovely navy blue skirt that hugged her shapely hips. She combed her braid loose with her fingers and brushed her hair tangle-free until it glistened with a blue-black luster. She glanced in the mirror and remembered the way Joseph stared at her last night, seeing her hair down for the first time.

On an impulse, she decided to let it hang free but pulled small sections at her temples to the back and tied them together with a blue grosgrain ribbon. She pulled on her button-up boots and put her hand on the doorknob.

Suddenly doubt assailed her. Could she make Joseph fall in love with her? Is that what the Lord expected of her? She bit her bottom lip and prayed for strength and wisdom. Then she took a deep breath and opened the door in search of breakfast.

As she approached the dining room, she heard a deep male voice. That same smile tugged at her mouth, and she smoothed her skirt over her hips and entered the room.

She walked directly to Joseph's side and rested her hand on his sleeve. Mustering up the sweetest voice she could manage, she greeted him, "Good morning, sweetheart. You should have waked me," and she winked for only his eyes to see. Then in a swift move, she placed a moist kiss on his cheek and moved on to hug a smiling Emily.

Taking her seat on the other side of Joseph, she had to swallow a giggle. His eyes were huge, his face blanched white, and his mouth gaped open.

If he wants a happy marriage for his mother, I plan to give it to him! With that thought, Lydia let a giggle slip, much to Joseph's horror and Emily's delight.

Lydia felt exhilarated and ready to beat Joseph at his own game. She had a hearty appetite, while Joseph nibbled his food. She glowed with happiness, while Joseph grouched with misery. She giggled and laughed, while Joseph sighed and growled.

Emily complimented Lydia on her new outfit and the way she fixed her hair. At the mention of hair, Joseph choked on his coffee, and his face slightly blushed when he looked in her direction.

She grinned and batted her eyes at him. Then she brought half her hair over her shoulder to lie across her chest.

She locked blue eyes on his shocked brown ones and confessed, "I think Joseph likes my hair down better."

Emily's shining face was evidence of her happiness for the new couple. She said something about needing more coffee and excused herself.

As soon as she left the room, Joseph questioned Lydia in hushed tones, "What in the world do you think you are doing?" his eyes glaring with anger.

She whispered close to him, "I'm doing exactly what you asked, Joseph. This is the way married people—happily, married people act," she finished, seeing Emily headed back for the dining room.

"What are your plans for the day?" Emily asked, looking back and forth referring to them as a couple.

It was Lydia that answered first, "I was hoping Joseph would show me the ranch today."

"Oh, that's a wonderful idea, Joseph." Emily clapped in approval. "Lydia needs to choose her own horse too."

"Horse?" Lydia squeaked, "I ... I don't know ... I mean, I've never ..."

Emily looked shocked. "Lydia, my dear, you don't know how to ride?"

She shook her head and noticed a victorious grin on Joseph's face. He thought he would weasel out of this one, but Emily came to Lydia's rescue.

"Joseph, you must teach her to ride," she pinned Joseph with her convinced eyes. "I bought her a wonderful riding skirt yesterday assuming she knew how to ride."

Lydia stood to leave when Joseph found his tongue.

"I can't," he stated dryly, "I have work to do."

"Nonsense," Emily retorted, "you may not have been able to travel on a wedding trip, but I insist you take a day or two to yourselves. Why, you're just getting to know each other."

Joseph stifled the growl that pulled up a corner of his mouth. He stood to his full height and puffed out his chest. "I can't take the time until Thursday or Friday. I've got strays to roundup and calves to brand."

Lydia watched as Joseph moved to his mother's side and dropped a kiss on her cheek. When he stood, she cast hopeful on eyes on him. She expected a kiss too. He released a huge sigh, and he moved toward her, but she playfully side-stepped him and giggled.

"Joseph, you owe me two since you kissed your mother first." She pouted and winked at Emily, who laughed in agreement.

"Forgive him, Lydia, he has to get used to the idea of a wife." Emily laughed again.

Joseph wagged his head from woman to woman and shook his head in frustration. Then Lydia saw his lopsided grin appear, and the thought floated through her mind that he looked like a mischievous child.

In several quick strides, he was at her side with a cheeky grin that scared her. She backed away from him, but not fast enough. His long arms caught her by the waist and reeled her in tight to his chest.

He bent low to whisper into her ear, "You're playing with fire, Missy." Then his lips covered hers for the first time in a sweet kiss. He

81

drew back far enough to see her stunned face, then dropped a quick kiss on her cheek.

"And that makes two." He winked and strolled out of the house.

Titus pawed the ground impatiently, ready to exercise his powerful legs, but the cowboy that mounted him sat still, thinking.

I knew I should have lit out for the range! It's the only safe place for me. The range, my men, and my herd! Who does Mother think she is ordering me to teach Lydia to ride? Take off two days from my work, huh! I am the head of this ranch, and I will decide when I can take days off!

Women! I thought it was bad enough with Mother. But now I have Lydia too. I sure have done it this time. And then I went and kissed her. I kissed her? Why did I do a fool thing like that? Because she asked for it, that's why! The little imp thinks she can outsmart me. I'll show her, if I want to kiss her I will, and anytime I want to, after all she is my wife! Besides, there is no way I'm going to have two women run my life!

Joseph smacked himself in the head. "What am I thinking, Titus?" Joseph spoke out loud, bewildered by his feelings. "I can't just be kissing on my wife anytime I want." He pushed his Stetson back and wearily rubbed his throbbing forehead.

He urged Titus out of the yard and into the open range at a smooth canter, enjoying the wind in his face. The morning was warming already, and he tried to think of the day ahead, but long flowing, black tresses filled his thoughts. It was crystal blue eyes and tender lips that caused his heart to twist and pulled his mouth into a lopsided smile.

Her lips were as sweet as honey. My fingers are longing to trickle through that silky, black hair. I declare, she is a tempting little imp.

A wide smile transformed his sun-tanned face as he nudged the giant horse into a gallop. That smile was still in place as Joseph reined Titus in beside his foreman Buck Hanson on the rise overlooking the partial herd.

"Mornin', Boss."

"Good morning, Buck. How'd everything go last night?" Joseph questioned, looking over the long horns.

"Fine, just fine. I had three men on night watch, and everything was real nice and quiet."

"Good, just the way I like it," Joseph replied. "How many men does that give us for the day?"

"Well, the three that kept night watch will bed down for a while, and that will leave us five men, six counting you."

"I think four of us should be able to roundup the rest of the strays today, while we leave two men watching the herd right here. I would like to start branding at sunrise tomorrow," Joseph informed Buck. "Doesn't Shorty ride the best cutter?"

"Yes," Buck hesitated.

Joseph turned his eyes from the herd and wondered what caused the hesitancy in his foreman's voice.

"Is there a problem, Buck?

"Well, you remember Shorty got hitched a little over a week ago."

"Yep, I remember."

"He's living in town now with his wife, and he hasn't been coming in until we finish with our breakfast," Buck finished lamely, unsure of the way Joseph would handle the news.

Joseph milked his square jaw and turned squinted eyes back to the herd. He couldn't blame the man for wanting to be with his wife, but it was more convenient for the ranch hands to live on the premises. He shifted in the saddle when a thought hit him.

"I wonder," Joseph thought out loud, "I wonder if Shorty and his wife would consider living on the Circle B? Remember that cabin in the north forty that we bought from old man Winston? I'm sure it would need some fixing up, but at least he would be closer."

"You know, it might not be a bad idea to have someone over that way, what with the trouble an' all," added Buck.

"You're right. Where is Shorty?" Joseph asked, straining his vision to identify the riders on the range. "I think I'll talk to him about it right away."

When Shorty Lawson heard his boss's proposition, he jumped at it. He hated living in town and longed to get back to ranch life. Shorty assured Joseph that he would make any needed repairs on the cabin and watch over that corner of the ranch.

Joseph mentioned that branding began in the morning, and he would need Shorty to begin cutting out the calves at first light. He suggested that Shorty take off after the rest of the strays were rounded up and talk it over with his wife. Then the two of them could come in the morning for breakfast. Afterward Susie could see the place and spend the day at the ranch with Lydia and his mother.

After a leisurely second cup of coffee, Lydia excused herself from the breakfast table. Once in her room, she was surprised to see that Joseph must have come back here to put the bed back together. Of course, he didn't want his mother to see their sleeping arrangements and figured she wouldn't have thought of it. But she would remember from now on; in fact, she planned to be the perfect, little wife.

In just the matter of a few days, she had to acquaint herself with yet another bedroom in the Banister home. This room was much larger than the guest room in which she had stayed.

The walls were papered light green and the curtains were forest green brocade with gold braided accents. Several oval rugs with large gold and pink roses were scattered on the hard wood floor. There was a large fireplace to the right of the entrance and a small green velvet couch and matching chair. The table beside the straight-backed chair had a lovely lamp on it. Most of the room hinted to a woman's touch, and Lydia wondered if this hadn't been his parents' bedroom. She moved about the room, running her hands over the beautiful furniture, unable to believe this was her room now.

She snuggled down on the small couch and smiled. She hugged herself and traced her lips with a finger, the very lips that Joseph had kissed. She could still feel the tingling sensation in them and the breathless way his touch left her.

There was hope; she had seen it in his eyes several times. She was sure of his interest before the marriage, and that kiss proved it was still there. He just didn't know it yet, and it was her job to help him see it.

She wondered if the things Joseph had told her about his father were true. She bit her lip trying to figure out a way to approach the subject with Emily without raising any suspicions. She snapped her fingers when she had the perfect idea and went in search of Emily.

It was just as she had hoped; Emily was at the clothesline helping Maria hang the daily wash. Lydia strolled up beside her and began to help, purposely choosing a pair of Joseph's jeans.

She held them high and gave a low whistle. "He sure is a big man," she commented to Emily and smiled.

"Yes, he is, took back after his father."

Using deft hands, she hung the huge pair of jeans and reached for a shirt, before innocently asking, "What was Joseph's father like?"

"Oh, much like Joseph, I guess," Emily said, then looked beyond the clothesline to another day.

Lydia continued to hang clothes, feeling sure Emily would go on with her description of Joseph's father.

When Emily reached for another piece of clothing, the basket and Maria were gone, and Lydia stood waiting for her to come back from the memories she had visited.

"Well, that went by quickly," she recovered and took Lydia by the arm. She suggested, "Why don't we take something cool to drink onto the patio, and I'll tell you all about him."

Lydia listened the rest of the morning as Emily told her about Joseph's father. He had been a tall, dashing young man when they first met at church. He had only recently been saved and attending church when he asked Emily's father if he could call on her. Emily was thrilled, and Richard swept her off her feet. He was an answer to her dreams. They married just months after and headed west to the territories.

Emily didn't mind the move as much as she minded the company. Richard was such a different man when he was with his parents. His father held a strong sway over him, and most of the time, it was not for the better.

Emily confided in Lydia that she doubted if the older Banister had ever been converted, but she had never voiced her uncertainty to anyone else. The sad thing about it was that Richard thought his father was a godly example and mimicked his every action.

Life was hard. While the men worked at building a herd and raising food for the family, the women worked every minute at just existing. The little soddy that they lived in was small, damp, and filled with bugs. It held the smoke from the old woodstove, and when it rained, it leaked, causing mud to fall into their food.

While the men hunted for meat, the women kept up the livestock. Washing clothes was tortuous, and drying them in the cold, damp winter was worse.

But Emily told Lydia the hardships of living were not as difficult to handle as were the changes in her Richard. He believed his parents' marriage was the example for his own, which broke Emily's heart.

Richard soon treated her as badly as his father treated his wife. Daily she witnessed him become his father, and she was unable to do anything but pray.

Emily admitted that things were not always so bad. It was the little things that Richard did that helped her through the tough times. When his father wasn't around, she was able to bring the best out in Richard. The nights were filled with whispered vows of love and promise, and in the rare moments when they were to themselves, Richard showed her the kind of man he could be without the influence of this father.

Emily had prayed that one day they would have their own place, and life would be sweet again. But that was not her father-in-law's idea. When they built their first cabin, it was a two-family dwelling. And little by little, Emily realized she was losing her Richard.

Her salvation came in the form of a sweet little boy named Joseph. He was the joy of her life, and she loved him to distraction. Richard loved him too and was so proud to have a son to carry on the Banister name.

As the herd grew, it afforded them a better life. Once again Emily hoped they could build a home of their own, but by now Richard was his father. The bitter, old man had completely corrupted Richard's way of thinking toward his wife—a wife was to serve and keep silent. She was to take any treatment her husband handed her and call it submission. He was the final authority in the home, and she had but to obey.

Of course, at that time there was no church or godly influence for Richard to know any better. But Emily knew what the Bible taught and tried to help Richard with a spiritual understanding of love, family, and their relationships, yet Richard's father's influence was too great.

As the area grew, the little church in town was started, and they attended, but by then, Richard believed he and his father had the right idea and that the Bible backed them up.

After Richard's father died, Emily prayed he would change. Many times she witnessed the Lord deal with Richard about his ill-temper and foul treatment of her, but he was unyielding.

Emily told Lydia she knew it was a choice that Richard had made for his life, and only he could change it. He mellowed a little but never confessed that his temper was a sin and committed the problem to the Lord.

He had been gone for several years, and Emily admitted that she missed him at times, especially when she remembered the good things, but she regretted that Richard never knew how sweet a marriage could be. That's why she had arranged things for Joseph. She wanted him to know the blessings of love and family.

Emily took Lydia's hands in her own and thanked her for being submissive to the Lord's will for her life, because she knew that the Lord had brought her to them. Already she could see a special look in her son's eyes, and she prayed their love would grow and blossom into a loving family.

After lunch, Lydia invited Emily to share in her devotions. The women spent the better part of the afternoon reading the Scriptures, praying, and sharing their testimonies. Each needed the other's company, and they grew from it.

Lydia knew Joseph wouldn't be home until late in the evening, and she wanted everything to be special for him. She made arrangements with Carlos to prepare a bath for Joseph (not knowing Emily had already done the same) and checked into making him a special pie.

Emily said that she didn't mind, but Lydia would have to wrestle it out with Maria. After quite a bit of persuasion, Maria gave her consent and shared her kitchen with Lydia. Before long, a juicy apple pie sat on the table cooling in the kitchen.

Then Lydia spent the early evening fussing over her hair and outfit. She settled on sweeping her hair into a loose bun and tied white lace around it. She chose a frilly, two-piece white suit out of the new clothes Emily bought the day before. The tailored shirt waist buttoned up the front with a sweetheart neckline edged in white lace and embroidered with white thread and small pearl beads. The sleeves were full to the elbow and fit tightly to the wrist. The skirt hugged her slim hips and fell into a full skirt to the floor.

She placed a clean shirt and jeans on the bed for Joseph and went into the living room to wait for his arrival. It was seven-thirty before she heard his horse outside. She made sure Carlos was filling the bathtub and went to the kitchen for a glass of lemonade.

JOSEPH RUBBED HIS EYES HARD to make sure he was awake and not just dreaming the beautiful woman standing at the door waiting for him. Too many times he had daydreamed this vision, but tonight it was real. Lydia stood in the doorway with the glass in her hand, waiting for Joseph to come in. She smiled brightly as he moved past her into the house.

"How was your ... your day, Joseph?" she fumbled.

Why did she have to be so beautiful? Why did she do the things I had always dreamed that a wife of mine would do?

But to Lydia, he just smiled that lopsided smile and answered, "Fine."

She followed him into the living room and placed his glass of lemonade on the table in front of the couch. He sat down and pulled his boots off and raised his stocking feet to the table.

She moved a chair and sat down, twisting her hands unconsciously. "Um ... did you get the cows ... um ... together?" she questioned, faltering for the correct terms.

He smiled at her attempts to pull him into a conversation. She was so lovely when she was unsure of herself. He noticed the way her hair billowed around her heart-shaped face and her crystal eyes flashed with frustration over her lack of knowledge. His eyes moved to her lips, caressing their fullness and remembering their delicious sweetness.

Startled by the memory, he glanced up to see her eyes on him, and a guilty pink blush overspread her face. Their eyes met for long moments, and each knew they had thought of the kiss they had shared earlier.

Joseph swiped his Stetson off his head and raked his fingers through his sweaty hair. He had to keep his mind in safe places.

"Yes," he was finally able to answer, "we rounded up the strays, and they will be ready to brand at daybreak."

"What is branding?" she wondered out loud. And she added, "I'm sorry, Joseph, I don't know anything about your cows." She quickly bowed her head and apologized again, "You don't need to answer. I'm sure it's none of my business."

Joseph wondered what made her feel that way, but he knew that he liked the idea that she wanted to know.

"Lydia," he called and waited until she looked at him, "Lydia, branding is a way of marking the beeves in your herd. Each rancher has his own mark that is burned into the hide of each one of his herd. Our brand is a Circle *B* created by my father and grandfather. It looks like this."

Joseph used his finger to trace an invisible capital *B* on the table and made a circle around it.

"We also cut two slits in the ears of each new calf that's branded. This is called earmarking a calf and is another way to show the calf belongs to our herd," he finished explaining.

"Does it hurt the calf?"

"I'm sure it does, but the branding iron is just the right temperature to cause a scab without permanently damaging the calf."

She smiled her brightest smile and moved behind Joseph, massaging his neck. At first he jumped with her touch and wanted her to stop, but soon his tired muscles relaxed and felt better.

"Thank you for explaining that to me, Joseph."

"You're welcome," he purred.

"There is a hot bath waiting for you, and supper will be ready soon," she informed him and patted his shoulder.

He stood to his full six feet and beamed that cheeky grin. "Yes, ma'am," he teased and bowed low.

"Oh, go on now"—she swiped a hand in his direction—"before I come to wash your back!"

Joseph's eyes grew with the suggestion, and he quickly turned to the hallway, hoping she was just teasing.

He entered the bedroom and smiled at the large tub of hot water and the clean clothes on the bed.

A fella could get use to this kind of spoiling. What am I saying? He hit his forehead. *She is the enemy, and if I don't keep that in mind, I will doom a son to the curse.*

With that thought, Joseph remembered his mother for the first time.

Emily heard Joseph's voice in the living room, and she moved into the hall to go greet him. She halted her steps when she heard Lydia's voice. She quietly sighed and decided to allow the young couple some time to themselves.

She turned to go back to her room when everything went silent in the living room. She inched up the hallway and peeked around the corner to witness the tender moment that passed between the newlyweds.

A smile broke across her face as she listened to their conversation begin again. She held her breath when she heard Lydia question Joseph over the ranch. For a moment, she wondered if Joseph would behave as his father had but found relief when she heard him patiently answering his wife's question.

She suspected he would not be like his father, but it was so good to have her suspicions confirmed. Happiness filled her heart as tears spilled down her cheeks, thankful that her son could experience the gift of love.

Joseph entered the dining room to find Lydia looking like an angel in her white suit and surrounded by the yellow glow of candlelight. His throat became dry and his heart stopped, then restarted at a gallop. He had never seen her lovelier. He was tired of playing the game already. But he must be strong if his plan was to work. He could not give in to his feelings of attraction to Lydia. He marched to the candles and blew them out.

"I'm tired and hungry. I just want to get this over with," he barked to the horror of the women.

"Joseph!" Emily snapped.

Lydia's eyes instantly watered with tears, and she ran from the room.

"Well! You've done it now, son. Lydia has worked around the house all afternoon trying to make things special for you," Emily accused, her voice full of irritation. "I hope you enjoy your dinner, alone. And be sure to have the apple pie that Lydia baked just for you. But be careful not to choke!"

Emily twirled on her heel and stormed from the room.

Slumping into his seat, he was disgusted with himself. For the sake of his plan, he had to do it. If he would have followed his feelings when he saw Lydia, he would have swept her up in his arms and carried her away.

He dropped his weary head into his hands and felt like weeping. This plan of his was not working. Instead of convincing his mother they had a happy marriage, he was hurting her and Lydia too.

When Maria entered the dining room, she found Joseph sitting by himself. She asked where the women had gone, and Joseph explained he would be dining alone and added that he just wanted a piece of pie.

Maria's black eyes flashed fire, and she stamped out of the room sputtering in Spanish.

Great, now I have all three women upset with me! Lord, I sure have made a mess of things. I guess I need your help more than I thought I did.

Joseph knew the pie was good, but he couldn't enjoy it. He knew what he had to do and dreaded it. Leaving the dining room, he went directly to his mother's room and tapped lightly on the door. Emily answered teary eyed and surprised to see him. At the sight of tears, Joseph's heart tightened until he couldn't breathe.

He reached out and pulled her into his embrace. "I'm sorry, Mother."

"I know, Joseph, but I am not the one to whom you should be apologizing."

He nodded against her hair and kissed the top of her head.

"Yes, I know," he sighed.

Releasing her, he plodded down the hall to his room. He tapped lightly on the door and called, "Lydia?"

From inside the room came a quiet voice bidding him to come in. She stood in her nightgown in front of the dresser, brushing long tresses of black hair. He could see in the mirror that her eyes were red and swollen and her nose a bright pink.

Joseph closed the door behind him and slipped up behind her. Taking the hair brush from her hand, he began to brush the beautiful hair he had been longing to touch. Even to his work-roughened hands it was deliciously silky. Stroke after stroke, he brushed in silence until her hair shined with a healthy luster.

When he stopped, he bent low and whispered in her ear, "Forgive me?"

She nodded her forgiveness and turned. Looking up into his brown eyes, she mischievously grinned. "You know I am not going to make this easy for you, Joseph," she firmly warned.

His eyes moved over her small face, and his heart raced in his chest, wondering if his foggy mind would ever clear again.

"So I see," he acknowledged with the lopsided grin.

She leaned in closer, daring him to capture her lips like he had this morning, but he stumbled away from her, raking his hand through his hair.

"Lydia, this can never work," he told her again, turning away from her. "I explained it all last night, and I thought that you understood."

As he spoke, he stepped away from her, unaware that she followed close behind him. He turned to see if she was listening when he stumbled into her and lost his balance. He grabbed her arms, hoping to steady himself, but instead, he took her down with him.

Twisting around before hitting the floor, Joseph avoided crushing her but landed hard on the floor.

Lydia was a ball of black hair and white cotton. She righted herself and moved to Joseph to be sure he was all right.

When he flashed a sheepish grin, she giggled herself and noted, "Joseph Banister, isn't this the way that I met you?"

Smoothing his furrowed brow with her hand and caressing his cheek, she added, "I believe you must have a hard time staying on your feet!"

"Why you," he growled and grabbed her wrists with his hands.

His chest thundered with his racing heartbeat, and his eyes moved over her full lips. They had been so sweet this morning, and the longing for them was so strong, but it was Lydia that lowered her lips to his in a peck and quickly escaped a stunned Joseph.

"Last one in the bed turns out the lights," she playfully challenged and slipped under the covers before Joseph scrambled to his feet.

"You little imp," he mumbled, remembering how he thought she was an impish temptress this morning, and now he was sure of it!

He blew the lamp out, shed his clothes, and climbed into his side of the divided bed.

"Good night, Joseph," Lydia's sweet voice floated across the bed.

He mumbled a good night but knew it would be anything but. This woman had him stirred in a way that he had never been stirred before, and he was quite sure it was dangerous.

They had lain in bed several silent minutes when Lydia's prayer once again broke the quiet. She prayed much like she had the night before and asked the Lord to bless their marriage and help her to be the kind of wife she should be to Joseph.

Guilt and conviction flooded his soul, but he pushed it aside, unwilling to face the truth.

Instead, he said to Lydia, "Good pie."

But to the Lord, he offered, "Help me, Lord, this was just day one."

13

JOSEPH JUMPED FROM THE BED well before dawn, remembering that the Lawsons were due for breakfast and he had not told a soul. He lit the lamp turning it low, grabbed his clothes, and leaned over the board to awaken Lydia.

She had forgotten to braid her hair last night, and it lay fanned across her pillow with her long eyelashes caressing her cheeks. Even in sleep she was a beauty, and Joseph sighed thinking he would like to watch her sleep but knowing he had to wake her.

He called her several times but could not rouse her. He reached over and gently shook her shoulder finally getting her to stir. She opened her eyes slowly and smiled when she saw his face peeking over the board.

"I thought I was dreaming, and you were calling me," she whispered and touched his cheek.

He swallowed hard and admitted he wasn't strong enough to keep her at arm's length this early in the morning.

"A nightmare maybe, but believe me, I'm not dream material. You need to get up. Last night I forgot to tell you the Lawsons were coming for breakfast."

Her eyes jerked wide open, and she squealed, "Oh no, Joseph! Breakfast?"

"Yes, and before dawn. Shorty is my best cutter. I need him to start cutting out the calves at first light."

She screwed her face into a puzzled look.

"I'll explain later. Now, get up, you sleepyhead!" he ordered and threw his pillow at her.

The Banister household was thrown into a sudden uproar. And once again, three women were upset with Joseph. They warned him that if he ever *forgot* to inform them of company again he would be visiting in the bunkhouse!

Knowing when he was outnumbered, he held up his arms in surrender. While the women worked, he told them about his idea for the Lawsons to move into the old Winston cabin. Emily agreed it was a wonderful plan and told Lydia she would enjoy meeting Susie.

Breakfast was whipped up in a hurry and ready when Shorty and Susie arrived. Introductions were made; although, Joseph noticeably stumbled over the word *wife*, and Lydia soon got over the shock that Shorty was really taller than Joseph. Joseph was happy to see that Lydia and Susie became instant friends.

Joseph hurried through breakfast anxious to get to the branding. He swallowed his food almost whole and sped through any conversation. But his mood visibly changed when Juan came in and whispered something to him. His brown eyes took on a dark, cold stare, and he motioned for Shorty to follow him.

Once outside, Joseph could not hold his temper; he punched the side of the stable with his fist and began to pace. Shorty and Will gave their boss plenty of room to blow off steam, knowing Joseph had every right to be frustrated. Will had brought him news that during the night someone had stole into camp and loosened all the horses.

When the men woke to find their rides gone, they set out on foot in search of them. Old Shotgun found them in a draw not too far away, but when he tried to climb down the sides of the gully, he fell and broke his leg. He was out cold for a while, and when he came back around, he claimed he had been pushed.

Joseph had known Shotgun for a long time, being the oldest hand he had on the ranch, and he had never known him to lie. No, Joseph felt sure he had been intentionally pushed just as Rusty's cinch had been cut. The hairs on the back of his neck stood when he considered that someone was deliberately trying to endanger his men and shut down the operation of the Circle B.

Joseph kicked a rock across the yard, wondering who had his ranch in their sights. He tried to be a good neighbor to the other ranchers and couldn't imagine who would want to hurt the Circle B. Although they made a good living, his ranch was considered small, but the Circle B was no threat to anyone, unless someone was trying to buy up the smaller ranches.

Joseph pushed his Stetson back and scratched his head. He would check into these things with the sheriff in town, but until then, they had to get things together for branding.

He told Will and Shorty what he wanted done, and Will rode out with two extra horses from the stable and instructions for Buck. Shotgun would be taken to Dr. Sloan in town by Rusty and Emily. The men were to round up the horses and set things up for branding sometime in the late morning. Then Joseph and Shorty went in to talk to the women.

First, Joseph took his mother into his office and spoke to her. Behind a closed door, he rehearsed what had happened with Rusty and explained this morning's incident with Shotgun. He also shared his suspicions with her and asked if she would inform the sheriff in town. He wanted Rusty to go with her and help get Shotgun to the doctor.

Joseph knew his mother was shaken. She had worked so hard beside his father to help make the Circle B all that it was today. He encouraged her to pray the Lord would help them find out what was happening.

Emily jumped into action. She never went back through the dining room but used the office door that led into the yard. Rusty was already waiting with the buckboard to go pick up Shotgun and get him into the doctor.

Then Joseph spoke with Lydia and Susie, brushing off the incident as an accident and warned the women they were stuck with their husbands for the cabin tour. He tried to appear lighthearted while avoiding Lydia's eyes.

After several attempts to question him, he told Lydia that he had sent his mother to help with Shotgun. He could tell that she was determined to know exactly what happened.

The foursome loaded into the buggy, and Joseph headed the horses toward the north forty. The men sat in the front, while the women sat in the back. Neither woman thought it unusual that the men were wearing holsters since both were unacquainted with ranch life. Nor did they notice that Joseph had slipped his rifle into the front of the buggy, and it lay ready at Shorty's feet.

To Lydia and Susie, this was like a Sunday ride, getting out into the fresh air and seeing the countryside. Lydia still had not seen any of the ranch but what was right there at the house, and Susie had lived in town all her life. So the ride was of great interest to the women; although, the men felt differently.

Whereas the women chattered in conversation the whole trip, the men were keenly alert to every movement, searching all around them for anything out of place. They had discussed the possibility that trouble could be waiting for them, and each felt the responsibility of protecting his wife.

However, the men relaxed when they found the cabin undisturbed. Together the Banisters and the Lawsons carefully examined the cabin and were surprised to find that it needed little repair, just a good cleaning.

Joseph and Lydia moved out onto the porch to allow the Lawsons time to make plans for the move. He walked to the far end of the porch and stepped off, but Lydia stood on the wooden platform enjoying the extra height it afforded her.

Now they were eye level, and Lydia questioned Joseph about the things that were happening at the ranch. When he tried to minimize their importance, Lydia placed both hands on his cheeks to stop him.

"Joseph, you are a terrible liar. I know something is bothering you. I see it in your jaw," she emphasized by caressing his taut jaw line with her hand.

She begged, "Please tell me."

Stepping up onto the porch, Joseph placed his large hands on her tiny waist. He knew she would not let up until she had the truth. He had learned that much about Lydia.

"The accidents with Rusty and Shotgun were deliberate acts. Someone is out to hurt the ranch."

A shudder of fear passed through Lydia, and Joseph pulled her close to his chest. He held her gently as though she would break and whispered a promise into her hair, "I won't let anyone hurt you, Lydia."

Emily entered the sheriff's office to find the new sheriff leaned over working on the office safe.

"I'll be with you in just a moment. Have a seat," the sheriff offered. "I'm having a terrible time with this doggone contraption. Fifteen years as a Texas ranger didn't prepare me for this kind of work. No, sirree, I just had to leave what I knew. Couldn't be happy with rangering, had to have me some new challenges in the Territories."

The sheriff referred to a scrap of paper one more time, his fingers twisted and turned the combination on the safe without any success.

"Never have coddled to any of these newfangled gadgets. I say stick to the old paths. It were good enough for my pappy and his before him," he complained.

"I know exactly how you feel," Emily replied in her very sweet, feminine voice.

The sheriff jolted at the sound of the female persuasion in the office and bumped his head into the gun case above. He grabbed at his throbbing head and mumbled under his breath. One look at his visitor revealed a twinkle of humor in her dancing brown eyes.

"I hope you don't think a knock on the head is something to laugh about," the middle-aged man accused Emily.

"No, Sheriff, really I don't," Emily choked, swallowing another giggle and covering her mouth with a slender hand. "But you remind me of my son. He always gets a bad case of the clumsy nerves when a woman comes near."

Emily's smile brightened her whole face, and she sat back to watch the show. She was comfortable in this setting, having been around men all her life. She didn't try to put on a giddiness or play dumb like so many women did when they had to do business with the sheriff. She spoke her mind and wasn't ashamed of it. She never left her seat or flustered over him like a silly woman with leave of her senses. She remained calm and confident.

"Would you like me to get the doctor for your 'knock on the head'?" she bemused.

He smiled at the use of his own words. He openly looked her over. She knew she didn't dress like many women. She had been the wife of a rancher, and she dressed with practicality in mind. She wore well-worn cowboy boots, a brown riding skirt, a white shirtwaist, and a kid leather jacket; in her hands, she held a very small, light brown Stetson.

"No, thank you, ma'am. I'd just as soon suffer in peace," he teased her and flashed her a winsome smile.

"Very well. May I go on with my business then before you pass out on the floor from pain?" she tormented further with a glint in her eye.

"Of course, don't let this lump or my splitting headache stop you," he rebutted.

Her smile broadened with his dry humor, and she introduced herself and informed him of the trouble they had been having at the Circle B. He asked if he could come out to the ranch later, and she told him Joseph would be home after eight.

"I look forward to meeting your husband tonight, Mrs. Banister," he commented.

He did not fool her with his unspoken question. "Sheriff, if you wanted to know if I were married, why didn't you just ask?" she questioned with a coy grin.

"I must say, Mrs. Banister, you are a very unique woman."

"Thank you, Sheriff, I will take that as a compliment," her words rolled off her tongue as she exited the office, leaving behind a man more intrigued than ever.

"Hey, wait a minute," Spencer spoke into an empty room, "she didn't say whether she was married."

Emily Banister smiled as she walked along the boardwalk. The new sheriff of Clayton said he loved a challenge, and she hoped to be that challenge.

14

Dirk Cutter grinned smugly when he received word to report to the Circle B for work. It was a good thing he had grabbed a few hours of sleep after his escapades last night. He hated the fact he would actually have to work, but he believed it would be worth it.

Cutter ran his hand over his greasy, slicked-back hair. He would have to put out a little for the branding, but afterward his intentions were less wholesome. The image of a shapely, black-haired beauty popped into his head, and he spurred his pinto into a faster gallop.

Buck Hanson was all business when Cutter rode into branding camp. He gave Cutter the spiel that he probably gave every cowpoke employed by the Circle B. Cutter noted the high regard the foreman had as he spoke of the boss. Hanson told Cutter that the boss never asked a man to do a job he wouldn't do himself. Like today, the boss would do a little bit of everything. Because of that, the men at the ranch respected Joseph Banister, and he expected Cutter to show that respect. The older Mrs. Banister called it the circle. It was a special camaraderie on the ranch that Joseph created because he wanted loyalty.

Introductions to the rest of the hands were brief, and soon the men were cutting out the cows with unbranded calves. Once these were separated, the roper would use his lariat to rope the calf, while a flanker brought the calf down for branding. A team of flankers worked to render the calf powerless while the brander applied the Circle B brand to the new calf. The marker used his knife to cut two slits in the calf's ear and called out to the tally man, who kept a count for the records.

The men had a good start before Banister and another man rode up. The other man took Will's place cutting, and Banister called Hanson aside for a report on their progress.

Cutter watched the big man that everyone referred to as *Boss*. It just wasn't right that one man have so much. He envied the younger man and felt that he deserved just as much if not more since he figured he was older than this rancher. Then with a conceited grin, he admitted to himself that he was definitely the better man.

A sneer tugged his upper lip as he sized up the big man. Banister had about four to five inches on him, but what Cutter lacked in height, he made up for in cockiness. His ego was quite large and his know-how larger. Many a time a man called him out, whether it was a fistfight or a gunfight, thinking Cutter would play by the rules only to end up at the undertakers.

That's what made his life so beautiful; he feared nothing and no one. He did what he wanted, when he wanted, without argument. This time was no different. True, he was taking orders, but just for a time. When he had his plan worked out, there would be no more orders only—

"Cutter," Hanson growled, "that's the third time I called you. Come over here."

Cutter's sneer became an annoying twitch, almost as annoying as that Hanson fella. He was an arrogant, demanding cuss, and Cutter thought he would love to grind him into the ground. Just the thought made him smile and look a little friendlier as he approached the boss man.

"Cutter," Hanson almost snarled, "this is Mr. Banister, the owner of the Circle B."

Banister stretched his hand out as he welcomed the cowpoke, "Good to meet you. I appreciate you jumping right in on such short notice."

Cutter hated the nice guy routine, and it made his stomach lurch to think this pitiful specimen of a man owned that vivacious beauty, but all Cutter's thoughts were carefully kept to himself.

He heartily shook Banister's hand and played the grateful cowboy, thanking Banister for the opportunity to work and dismissed himself as if he couldn't wait to get back in the saddle.

For the rest of the day, Cutter kept one eye on Banister and the other on his work. He watched Banister pull on his chaps and work as one of the flankers, the brander, and even the marker. When everyone broke for lunch, Banister lined up in the midst of them and took his grub from Red, just like any other cowpoke. He wallowed in the dust and sipped his coffee from an old tin cup.

It was all too much for Cutter. The respect, the loyalty, the camaraderie disgusted him. In his world, a man lived for himself, never trusting or giving true loyalty to another. Oh, there was a temporary loyalty among the thieves of a gang, but never a true loyalty, the kind for which one would give his life.

No, in Cutter's world, real men were loners, because aligning oneself with another made one vulnerable. A real man never depended on anyone else. Only the weak, like Banister, needed others.

And now in the midst of this camp, Cutter added yet another reason to despise Joseph Banister.

Lydia needed a few precious moments to herself before she joined the other women for lunch. Something special happened at the cabin this morning. She could hardly believe it, but not voicing it made it no less true. She closed her eyes and tried to put herself back into the arms of Joseph standing there on the cabin porch. Then she had snuggled closer to his chest and felt the steady beat of his heart. She remembered the musty scent of his shaving cologne and wondered at the strength of his mighty arms. She felt safe then and now, and she knew he would protect her.

It was then she first knew that she loved Joseph. Although she had only known him for a matter of days, she loved him. Somehow the Lord had prepared her heart to accept him with all of his mistaken conceptions and his ridiculous conditions. She loved Joseph Banister.

She had tempted him sorely standing in his arms, tightening her arms around his chest. It was so unfair to tempt him that way before the Lord was able to help him understand the truth about his father and his temper. But she wanted to be a wife to Joseph in every meaning of the word, and she wasn't about to fight her attraction for him as she suspected he was fighting his for her. She would keep these new feelings to herself until she was able to share them with Joseph.

Lydia joined Susie and Emily for a leisurely lunch. The young women told Emily about the cabin and their plans for decorating it. The rest of the meal passed with talk of curtains, rugs, and husbands. The two young women were fast friends with so many things in common.

After lunch, it was decided to gather around the table in the patio garden for a time of Bible study. Lydia noticed the surprise on Susie's face and immediately began to pray for her new friend. Just as she did the day before, Lydia naturally seemed to take the lead in the afternoon devotions, welcoming the opportunity to share the Scriptures in a way that she had with her own mother.

"On my way to the cabin this morning, I was able to see the mountains in the distance, and I noticed how rocky the land is here in the foothills. Those rocks reminded me of a story in Exodus about the children of Israel.

"The Lord had delivered them out of the bondage in Egypt, and they traveled through a desert wilderness toward their land of promise. But along the way, they gave out of water and complained to Moses. He turned to the Lord for direction and was instructed to climb a rock in Mt. Horeb, and there the Lord would provide the needed water.

"Now mind you, there were millions of people in the Israelite camp, and it would take an awful lot of water to meet their needs. But Moses obeyed and did as the Lord had instructed him. He took his rod and smote the rock, and it broke forth with water.

"The water was a necessity of life for the people. With it they lived and without it they died. The Lord provided that life-giving water, but it was up to every individual to come and take of that water."

Lydia knew she had said a mouthful and hoped that she had not lost Emily or Susie but was delighted to find she had their full attention.

She continued, "But that rock was special and the Apostle Paul later explained it in First Corinthians chapter ten. He said the *rock* was Christ. Not literally, of course," she added when eyebrows shot up in confusion.

"No, it was a beautiful picture of Jesus Christ. The Israelite story is an example filled with helpful truths for us. Now try to follow this. Our preacher in St. Louis showed it to us. Jesus was that *rock* that was smitten to give us the waters of life.

"Remember there was no water until Moses smote the rock, and that's just like Jesus. He had to be smitten, or crucified on the cross before He could provide us with the *water* of everlasting life. And now the *water* has been provided, but it is up to each of us to partake of it. And just like with the Israelites, if we have the *water* we live, that means we have everlasting life with God. But if we choose not to take the *water* that has been provided by Christ, we will die."

Preparations were made for a late dinner, and the women were ready when the dusty, weary men came home. Lydia had a glass of lemonade in her hand and greeted Joseph at the door as she had the night before. As Joseph entered, he dropped a kiss on her cheek without giving it a thought and dragged himself into the living room.

Susie had followed suit and greeted Shorty in the same way, and they followed the Banisters into the living room. The four discussed the day's events as the men pulled off hot boots and finished their lemonade.

Since branding had to be continued the next morning, Shorty and Susie were invited to spend the night and were shown to the guest room to freshen up. Lydia reminded Joseph of his bath and hurried him along with the promise of a delicious meal afterward.

Emily stood in the shadows as she watched Lydia arrange the meal and wait patiently for Joseph. Once again, Emily stayed in her room trying not to feel left out. She was so happy for Joseph and Lydia but had no idea that she would feel as if she were in the way. She remembered how she had hoped that she and Richard would have a home of their own and wondered if Lydia would feel that way too. This was a part of her plan she had not considered, and she knew that she must make some hard decisions in the days ahead.

The dining room was full tonight, and everyone enjoyed the meal and fellowship. Promptly at eight o'clock, the sheriff arrived to speak to Joseph. Emily made the introductions and invited him to share cake and coffee before speaking to Joseph. Spencer accepted the invitation and was seated next to Emily.

While dessert was served, Emily spoke up, "Sheriff, it's good to see you can tell time."

Joseph choked on his coffee and joined the others around the table in staring at Emily.

"Well, thank you, Mrs. Banister," Spencer replied with a smile tugging at the corners of his mouth, "it weren't easy since I had to follow the directions you didn't give me."

This time, eyes shifted to the sheriff, shocked that the man would be so bold to speak to Emily that way. Emily countered, "I wasn't sure you could read!" and a wide smile spread across her face.

Despite himself, Spencer could not hold his laughter, and Emily joined him, while four sets of eyes sat dumbfounded.

"Well, Mrs. Banister," he answered when he finally gained control of himself, "you've got me again."

Joseph and Lydia exchanged puzzled looks. But Emily's eyes shined with the wonderful banter.

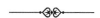

Joseph was too tired to think straight. After dessert, he spoke to the sheriff and was assured that the lawman would do what he could to help. Shorty, Susie, and his mother quickly excused themselves and retired to their rooms. Joseph just wanted to quietly fall into his bed and sleep.

Then he looked at Lydia. She smiled bashfully and took him by the hand. He was unable to fight her as she pulled his giant frame down the hallway and into their room.

She guided him to the small couch and ordered him to sit. She quickly fixed the board in the bed and changed into her night-gown. While she brushed and braided her hair, she warned Joseph not to fall asleep, because she would never be able to move him from the couch.

His eyes snapped open, and he had to jiggle around to keep himself awake. Lydia climbed into the covers and called for Joseph to turn out the light. He gladly complied and shrugged out of his clothes and into his side of the bed.

He heard Lydia's sweet good night and began to drift off to sleep. Before blessed slumber claimed him, he could hear Lydia's prayer for their marriage.

15

A<small>FTER</small> J<small>OSEPH AND</small> S<small>HORTY LEFT</small> to finish the branding, Rusty escorted Lydia and Susie into town to pack up the Lawsons' belongings. They also went to Evan's Mercantile for curtain material. The women planned on sewing up the curtains this morning and cleaning the cabin this afternoon. It was Susie's goal to have things settled enough to stay there that night.

The women shared a hurried lunch, and afterward Rusty drove the loaded wagon and the young women to the cabin. Even with a broken arm, Rusty was a big help. The cabin was completely emptied, dusted, swept, and washed down.

The late afternoon sun shone through gleaming windows as Lydia and Susie hung the new curtains. Rusty helped move the few pieces of furniture back into place, and Susie arranged a few colorful rag rugs. Dishes, food tins, and crocks were placed on the shelves in the small kitchen.

Three exhausted young people sat down to catch their breath, satisfied that the Lawson's new home was ready for them.

Lydia and Susie expressed their gratefulness to Rusty for all his help. He blushed with all the attention, waving off any further mention of it, but Lydia secretly decided she would reward him with some baked goodies.

Emily stayed home to work on the bookkeeping for Joseph. After two hours of addition and subtraction, she needed a break and decided to take a glass of lemonade onto the patio. In the heat of the day, the patio furnished a shady hiatus. The combination of the house walls and the lush greenery created a cool sanctuary. Emily had fought hard for this beautiful spot, and every day it gave her pleasure.

But when she entered her favorite place, a stranger was poking around the garden. Her appearance had startled him as much as his appearance had startled her, but he soon recovered and slowly approached her.

He was not the kind of man that was usually around the Circle B. He was a smaller man with slick, shiny hair. His eyes were narrow and dark, sending a shiver down Emily's back. He glared at her, and his eyes roamed over her body with a worldly desire.

The older woman was shocked with his boldness. For the first time in years, Emily was afraid in her own house. Her heart skipped beats and then thundered in her chest. She felt this stranger had violated her home and her person, and she wanted him out!

But she was frozen to the spot and hated herself for this powerless feeling. He swaggered across the patio toward her, never moving his eyes from her face.

Then a drop of condensation from the glass in her hand trickled over her white knuckles and shifted her thoughts long enough for her to gain control of her face. She altered her stance to a more aggressive position and glared back at the intruder. Her chin rose slightly, and she took a deep breath. This was her home, and he was not welcome!

"What are you doing here?" she hissed. Emily's keen eye noticed the way he tried to cover his arrogance.

"Excuse me, ma'am," he humbly apologized. "I hope I didn't scare you. I'm looking for the boss man."

Emily's nostrils flared at his attempt to be civil. "You work here?" she questioned, unable to keep the shock from her voice.

A sneer quickly passed across his face. "Yes, ma'am, replaced some fella that busted up his leg."

The sneer was replaced with a hint of a smile, and once again, a shiver passed through Emily.

"Your boss is branding, exactly where you should be."

He snarled, "Oh, that's right." And he turned and ambled from the garden.

Emily stood on her feet until she heard his horse clomp out of the yard, then collapsed on a bench. Her hand was shaking so severely she spilled lemonade on her skirt. She swallowed and tried to capture her speeding heart. Her trembling hand set the glass on the patio floor, and she dropped her head into her hands and wept.

Emily was in her room by the time Lydia and Rusty returned from the Lawson's cabin. Lydia checked with Maria when she didn't see Emily. Maria told her she had gone to lie down, so Lydia went to her own room to clean up.

Lydia saw to Joseph's bath, laid out his clothes, checked on dinner, and stood in the doorway with a cool glass of lemonade. She smiled brightly, greeting Joseph and Shorty, and reported to Shorty that Susie was settled in the cabin and waiting for him. He thanked her and Joseph once again for the cabin and headed his mount to the north.

Joseph slid from Titus and handed Juan the reins. He quietly thanked the stableboy while he slipped out of his dusty chaps and handed them over too.

Lydia covered a giggle as she watched his long legs wobble, having been in the saddle all day. He was dusty and sweaty but managed a smile for her.

"Hey, there cowboy," she teased calling from the doorway, "how about a cool drink, hot bath, and delicious meal?"

He smiled again when he saw the glass in her hand. He rambled toward her on sore, weary legs; dropped a wet kiss on her cheek; and claimed the glass from her hand. With his free hand, he reached around her waist, and together they walked into the living room.

Her breath caught with his touch, and her pulse sped up. She could hardly believe he held her this way but hoped he would never let her go.

Dropping his arm from her waist, he moved around the couch, set his glass down on the table, and flopped into the leather seat. His head wearily fell back, and his eyes closed. She quietly sat in the chair next to the couch and watched him. Even though he was dirty and smelly, she loved him. Minutes passed before his hat fell off his head and hit the floor behind the couch, causing him to slowly open one eye.

"Have I been asleep?"

"Not for long," she grinned.

"I'm sorry," he admitted and reached for her hand.

She reached out her arm to his, and he took her slender hand, pulling her to the couch. He stretched his legs out onto the table and was stunned to find his boots hit the wood.

"I forgot to take off my boots," he meekly confessed with a lopsided smile.

Then he released Lydia's hand to remove them, but to her surprise, he leaned back and recaptured her hand. His head fell to the side and rested on her shoulder. Never had she experienced this kind of stirring. Her breathing was coming out in short, little gasps, and every part of her body that touched Joseph tingled.

She whispered just in case he had fallen asleep, "Did you get the calves all marked up?"

A cheeky grin covered his face, and he peeked around to see her innocent smile.

"Yep," he answered, never correcting her.

Reaching up with her hand, she brushed the thick hair out of his eyes.

"I know you're very tired. Do you feel up to a bath and dinner?"

He nodded wearily. Pulling up in the seat, he grabbed his glass, and in several gulps, it disappeared. He stood and pulled her up within inches of his chest.

"I will take a quick bath and meet you in the dining room," he promised. And he added, "I'm starved!"

He dropped another wet kiss on her cheek and padded toward the hallway.

Lydia hugged herself and spun around the room. Since he was in such a pleasant mood, she would tell him tonight.

Joseph had just slipped into his jeans when a light knock sounded at the door. He grabbed his shirt to cover his bare chest, then threw it down on the bed. He cracked the door and was surprised to see his mother standing in the hall. He grabbed his shirt up again and shoved his arms into it, opening the door at the same time. She moved into the room without a word and went to sit on the couch.

He closed the door and began to button his shirt, taking the seat closest to her. It was evident that she had been crying, and his chest tightened with tension.

Reaching out his hand, he quizzed, "Mother, what's wrong?"

She looked terrible, her eyes and nose a bright red. She patted his hand and told him about the stranger on the patio. She sniffled as she explained how frightened he had made her and questioned if he worked for the Circle B.

Sneering, Joseph's thoughts settled on one man, Cutter.

"Yes, if it's who I think it is. Buck hired him yesterday to fill in for Shotgun."

Her eyes widen. "That's exactly what he said," she whispered, horrified that such a man was working for their ranch, and she told him as much.

"Don't worry, Mother," he vowed, "I will take care if this right away," and he patted her hand reassuringly.

He tucked his shirt in and offered his arm to escort her to dinner.

Dinner had been quiet, and Joseph left as soon as he finished eating. Emily pleaded a headache and left Lydia sitting alone in the dining room. She wondered what had happened to Joseph's wonderful mood as she pushed her chair back and moved toward their room.

She changed in silence and brushed her hair to ready for bed. She began to braid her hair when Joseph called from the hall.

She peeked around through a crack in the door and asked, "Do I know you?"

"I'm afraid so," he responded dryly.

She sighed, opening the door. He stepped into the room, preoccupied. She would have to wait to tell him. She fixed the board and slipped into bed.

He silently turned out the lamp, undressed, and crawled into his side of the bed.

Suddenly Lydia changed her mind. "Joseph," she paused, "I love you."

Joseph's eyes jerked open wide, and he couldn't believe what he had heard. Hadn't he told her this could never happen? Didn't she understand that he could never love her? This went beyond the love for his mother; this was about loving a wife—his wife now and a son he should never have.

His fist cracked the board between them, and Lydia jumped and cried out. Without lighting the lamp, he stomped over to her side of the bed.

Leaning toward her until his nose almost touched hers, he hissed, "I told you this is not for real! It can't be, don't you understand!"

Through the dark, she could see the veins in his neck bulged in anger. He grabbed her shaking shoulders and lifted her to a sitting position in the bed.

"Lydia," he milked his chin and started again, "I'm sorry this has gone as far as it has, but you must believe me. This marriage is a fake. It can never be a real marriage, nor can I ever fall in love with you."

He threw her back to the bed and grabbed his pants and shirt from the couch before he slipped out into the hall.

16

LONG INTO THE NIGHT LYDIA waited his return, but Joseph never came back.

The next morning, exhausted and discouraged, Lydia crawled from her bed. She spent some time on her knees praying the Lord would show her how she could help Joseph to understand. Once again, only peace came to her heart, and she took strength in knowing the Lord had brought her here and would not forsake her when she needed Him the most. He would provide for her even in the wilderness of New Mexico, just as He did for the children of Israel so long ago. She had to be patient and strong and believe the Lord would work with Joseph's heart.

She dressed for breakfast and pinned her hair into a loose bun. The branding was finished, and the herd had been returned to grazing, allowing Joseph to be at home today.

She remembered the warning she gave him just days ago, that she was not going to make this easy for him, and she meant it.

Marching to the dining room with a new determination, Lydia was going to find a way to make her husband fall in love with her!

Joseph and Emily were already at the table when she entered the room. She glided across the floor as if they had had a normal night and bid Joseph a good morning with a big, juicy kiss on his cheek.

Stunned, he growled his displeasure and mumbled under his breath.

114

"My, my, Joseph," his mother commented, "aren't we in a wonderful mood this morning."

Lydia stifled a giggle and knew that Emily would unknowingly be a fellow conspirator.

She seated herself and smiled at Emily. "Oh, don't mind him, he woke up on the wrong side of the bed," and Lydia flashed Joseph the sweetest grin she could muster.

He growled again, but the women chose to ignore his bad manners and continued a conversation between them.

"Lydia, I've been planning to talk to you, but things have been so busy around here."

"Yes, I know we hardly had any time together yesterday."

"I would like it very much, if you felt comfortable that is"— Emily paused and smiled—"if you would call me *Mother*."

Tears sprang into Lydia's eyes and threatened to fall. She nodded and swallowed hard but couldn't speak.

"Now don't you start that," Emily admonished, fighting her own tears.

Lydia sniffled back her tears. "May I call you *Mama*, like I called my—" she was unable to finish, and both women burst out in tears.

Joseph combed his hand through his hair, and a giant sigh escaped his lips. Suddenly Emily giggled, and Lydia joined her as they realized how uncomfortable Joseph had become.

"Lydia?" Emily laughed through her tears.

"Yes, Mama," Lydia responded using her new name for Emily.

"I think Joseph is about to blow. We had better dry it up before he loses it." Emily laughed at her own joke.

They dabbed their eyes, and Emily patted her son's hand. "Really, Joseph, you are quite the grouch this morning."

He remained sullen throughout breakfast; although, Lydia and Emily carried on a lively conversation about the Lawson's cabin and Lydia's budding friendship with Susie.

Emily swallowed her last bite of food and looked toward Joseph.

"Well, Joseph, I believe today is the day," she offered.

He narrowed his eyes and but made no comment.

Even though Joseph showed no interest in Emily's comment, she continued, "Today you will teach your wife how to ride!" she firmly ordered.

He shook his head, but Emily wasn't taking *no* for an answer.

Lydia tried to side with Joseph, pleading some trivial work needed to be done. She feared that Emily had picked up on the unspoken tension between them and thought to help them out.

Emily set her jaw in a stubborn fashion and crossed her arms over her chest. It was clear to see where Joseph got his stubborn streak. Emily looked from Lydia to Joseph and lifted an accusing finger.

"You promised her days ago, and a man is only as good as his word."

When Emily was like this, Lydia feared there was no winning. Joseph sighed and pushed his chair back, a defeated man.

He looked at Lydia and commanded, "Come on, or I'll not have a minute's peace today," and glared at his mother.

Lydia looked to Emily for help but was given a nod and a wink. Lydia hurried to her room and changed into her riding skirt and boots.

Once the silent couple was out in the yard, Lydia spoke, "This was not my idea, Joseph. And I'll understand perfectly if you don't want to teach me."

"I'm stuck," he countered, facing her with his hands on his hips. "But I don't have to like it."

He stalked into the stable, and she followed close on his heels. In spite of herself, she smiled and noted that sometimes he could really be a grizzly bear, but at other times, he was just a cuddly, little cub.

He stopped in front of a stall and began saddling up a beautiful chestnut-colored horse. He told Lydia that she was gentle and should make her a good mount.

"Are you giving me this horse?" she pondered, unable to believe her ears.

"Yes, Lydia," he responded dryly.

Jumping up beside him, she pecked a small kiss to his cheek and breathed. "Oh, Joseph, thank you."

A small grin tugged at the corner of his mouth, but he quickly hid it. They moved out into a corralled area, and he questioned her.

"Do you know anything about horses?"

She wagged her head and admitted in a small voice, "No."

He briefly explained the parts of a horse and the saddle with which she needed to be familiar. He spoke as if he were bored with the whole project, and Lydia was beginning to feel like a terrible burden.

Moving a feed bucket to the left side of the horse, Joseph motioned for her to come forward. He explained that she was to step up on the bucket, place her left foot in the stirrup, while swinging her right foot over the horse's back, bringing herself into the saddle.

She wanted to please Joseph so much that when she swung her leg around, she used too much force and flipped right over the horse and onto the ground with a thud.

Joseph crossed his arms over his chest and turned his smiling face in another direction but never offered to help her or run to her side. This riled Lydia more than anything he had done or said so far.

What nerve! He just stood there ignoring the fact that she was sprawled out on the ground. She jumped up with fire in her eyes and stomped back around the horse.

"Joseph Banister, I am tired of playing your stupid game! I know good and well this is not about teaching me to ride this animal," she accused, pointing to the innocent horse.

She stepped up onto the bucket again and faced Joseph eye to eye. Reaching her arms around his neck, she kissed his lips and whispered, "I love you, Joseph, and I want a real marriage."

Her eyes begged him to give in, but he pulled her arms from around him, screaming, "No!"

Lydia fell off the bucket and stomped off in a huff toward the stables; Joseph kicked the bucket, sending it sailing across the dirt and crashing into the fence.

He stormed from the corral and headed for his office door to escape Lydia, his mother, and the whole world!

Lydia stumbled into the stable, blinded by her tears. Joseph had made her madder than she could ever remember being. She found an empty stall and plopped herself onto a pile of hay for a good cry.

Cutter didn't care whether Buck Hanson had fired him or not. He had come for a purpose and was not leaving without the woman. He had hid himself in the stable last night after the foreman told him to grab his gear and leave. He had been hiding there when Banister stalked into the stables and slept with his horse.

This morning, he stayed hidden and waited for a good time to search for his prize. He was surprised to find that she was being brought to him!

He heard Banister give her the horse and then call her by name. "Lydia."

The name suited her, thinking it sounded rare and beautiful.

He peered through the slats of the stable and watched the big man explain how to mount the horse he had saddled for her. Cutter sneered when she fell, and Banister would not even lift a hand to help her up. His treatment of Lydia was beyond belief and only helped Cutter justify his desire to take her from this man.

He witnessed her attempt to reason something with him and how she threw herself at him only to be pushed away. Cutter's eyes grew large, and hate rose in his throat. One day he would give Joseph Banister exactly what he had coming to him.

Then to Cutter's surprise, Lydia headed for the stables as Banister went in the direction of the house.

A sly grin formed across his face, and he peered around his stall to see where Lydia went. He licked his lips and slicked his hair back into place, feeling that lady luck was shining on him today.

He stole his way to her stall and found her crying on a pile of hay.

"Lydia, you need a real man," he proposed.

Lydia's head jerked up to find a stranger hovering over her. She cowered back against the wall of the stall in fear.

He pulled her up by her shoulders, delighting in her soft skin. He inhaled deeply of her perfume and stared into her crystal blue eyes.

"I won't hurt you like he did, so don't even think about screaming," he warned in hushed tones.

Shaking with fear, she nodded in compliance.

His finger traced her cheek and traveled down her neck.

"You are more beautiful than I thought," he grinned, his eyes moving to her hair.

He leaned against her, pinning her tightly to the wall. Then he reached up and pulled the pins from her hair, allowing it to fall about her shoulders. He ran his fingers through her thick tresses and smiled lustfully into her eyes.

"I've seen the way he treats you. He doesn't deserve a woman of your rare beauty."

He ignored the look of fear in her eyes and the tears that rolled down her cheeks. He moved a hand down the side of her slim body and whispered, "I promise you I will be good to you," and a wicked laugh split the quietness.

"Please, no," she was finally able to say.

He gripped her chin in his hand and lowered his head to kiss her, but she moved her face to the side to escape his lips.

Angered, he hauled back his hand and slapped her across the face, making her cry out in pain. Blood trickled from her split lip, and he used a fingertip to wipe it away.

He lifted her chin to peer into her eyes and cautioned, "Don't pull away from me again."

Joseph stalked toward the office grumbling over the horrible events of the morning. And to think that his mother had sided with Lydia!

"Just call me *Mother*," he grumbled, mocking his mother's request to Lydia.

Great, just great, Mother! She loves you, she loves me, and now she's going to think of you as her own mother! I'm doomed! And the tears! Both women crying at the same time! It was all too much! I can't take much more of this. After all, I spent the night in the barn with my horse!

Joseph slammed through the door of his office and stopped short when his mother looked up from the desk in surprise. He raised his head in total frustration and blew out some pent-up air.

"Joseph! What have you done to Lydia?"

"Lydia," he hissed through clenched teeth. "Lydia, Lydia, Lydia!" he raged, each word getting louder and louder.

"Joseph Banister, you listen to me right now!" Pausing to get his attention, she rose from her seat and braced her arms on the desk. "Ever since Lydia came into our lives you have been nothing but a moody, mixed-up kid. And I want to know what is going on!" Now Emily's voice was just as loud as Joseph's had been.

He threw his hat into the corner of the room and stalked back and forth, knowing there was no way he could tell his mother the truth. He was not even sure he knew what the truth was anymore. He would have to settle for a half-truth.

Brushing his shaky fingers through his hair, he dug his thumbs into his belt and tried to calm down. His nostrils flared with each cleansing breath until he was finally able to speak in a normal tone.

"Don't worry about it, Mother," he lied. "It's just a lover's quarrel."

Leveling her brown eyes on him, she warned, "Joseph, don't you hurt that sweet girl. Now I don't know what you did, but I want you to turn yourself around, find her, and apologize."

She crossed her arms and waited for him to leave. Long minutes passed as they stood there staring at each other wondering who would give in. Before long, Joseph whirled on his heel and slammed out the door almost as he had come in.

Joseph used the distance between the house and the stable to think of a way out of this marriage. His plan had been a complete and total failure, and now he feared he would not be able to control his growing feelings for Lydia.

But there was more at stake than their feelings. If he could just get her to understand he was doing this for her protection. He didn't want her to know the rage that boiled inside him or feel his knuckles against her tender skin.

He loved her too much for that. The thought stopped him cold in his tracks. *Admit it, Joseph, you've loved her from the beginning. The moment those lovely blue eyes filled with concern at your falling into the dirt, you fell for her, and you've been falling deeper ever since.*

"Well, maybe so," he admitted into the air, "but that just means I will have to try harder to make my plan work!"

Several long strides had him to the door of the stables, and he squinted to adjust his eyes to the darker interior.

"Lydia," he called out, "where are you?"

Joseph stepped into the building, cooler than the outside this time of day and peered into a few stalls.

"Lydia, I'm sorry about blowing up like that," he hesitated, hoping she would peek around some stall.

He continued moving through the stable as he talked, "I want us to try to work things out."

When there was still no sign of her, his heart began to beat faster and his steps quicken. Stall after stall he checked until his search ended, and he was face-to-face with Cutter holding a knife to Lydia's throat.

THE MUSCLES IN JOSEPH'S BODY tensed when he saw the fear in her eyes and the blood on her lip. He promised himself that when Lydia was out of harm's way, he was going to take great pleasure in beating this worm to within an inch of his life.

"Don't take another step closer, Banister," threatened Cutter. "I never wanted to hurt Lydia, but I will if I have to." Cutter squeezed her closer to show Joseph he meant what he said.

Lydia's eyes begged Joseph to help her, sending fresh tears down her face.

Never had Joseph been so mad and so helpless all at the same time. If he moved, Cutter may slit her throat, but if he didn't, Joseph couldn't bear to consider what might happen.

"Now me and the lady here are just gonna move slowly out of the stall and get my horse so we can leave."

Joseph watched helplessly as Lydia's eyes flashed with terror at the suggestion of leaving with Cutter. The desperation was written all over her face as her eyes cut over to an object against the dividing wall of the stall. Joseph's eyes never left her face, but he remembered a shovel leaning there.

Suddenly Lydia grabbed at Cutter's face with her fingernails, scratching and gouging at his eyes. He hollered out in pain, dropping his grip on her, and she threw herself to the open end of the stall.

Joseph snatched up the shovel and swung it with all his might, knocking the knife from Cutter's hand and cracking his knuckles.

Before Cutter knew what hit him, Joseph swung again; this time with his fist making contact in Cutter's gut. As the intruder doubled over in pain, Joseph came up with a hard punch to his face, throwing him backward into the wall. Cutter hit with a sickening thump and sagged to the hay.

Gasping for breath, Joseph hovered over Cutter, hoping he would get up so Joseph could hit him again. His nostrils flared in hostility, and he dared Cutter breathlessly, "Don't you ever touch *my wife* again."

When Joseph was assured that the scoundrel had passed out, he hurried to Lydia. Scooping her up into his arms, he carried her out of the stable and away from Cutter.

As they walked, she latched her arms around his neck so tightly Joseph feared he would lose his breath. Trembling in his arms, she was a mass of long, black hair. She was crying again, and her tears were soaking his shirt.

In long strides, he took her through the patio and into their room successfully avoiding everyone. He closed the door and sat on the bed with her in his lap. He rocked her, whispering soothing words into her hair.

For long moments, she cried sometimes squeezing him tighter, but he didn't care because he had her safe in his arms. He whispered, long after she stopped crying, assuring her of his love and promising he would protect her.

She finally removed her arms from about his neck and raised her head. He brushed her damp hair out of her face with tender strokes. Then his fingers softly moved across her cheeks, wiping away her tears.

Their eyes held each other's as he carefully traced her split lip with a shaking finger.

"Did he hurt you anywhere else, sweetheart?"

She shook head *no*, but fresh tears trickled down her cheek.

He pulled her close to his thundering chest and whispered, "Oh, Lydia, I'm so sorry. I should have been there to protect you. I should have never blown up and left you there by yourself."

Lydia raised her head and touched her fingertips to his lips. "Shhh," she hushed him, "you had no idea that man was in there waiting for me."

Tears clouded Joseph's eyes for the first time when he realized he almost lost her. His hand cupped her soft cheek and tenderly kissed her forehead, then her nose, and on to her cheek. Her eyes closed at his touch.

In a husky voice, he breathed, "I love you, Lydia."

Then his lips brushed hers with a tender kiss. Carefully his lips moved from one side of her face to the other, gently leaving feather-light kisses in their wake. He longed to kiss her full on the lips with all the passion that was exploding in his chest, but he remembered her split lip.

They sat there in each other's embrace for quite a while until Joseph remembered he needed to get the sheriff for Cutter. Reluctantly, he released Lydia and scooped her up only to lay her on the bed again.

"I'm going to take care of Cutter. I'll send Mother in to see to that lip," he informed her. "Do not get up. I want you to rest until the sheriff comes."

He bent low and placed a tender kiss on her lips and slipped out the door.

Emily hurried to the room to check on Lydia. She could hardly believe such a thing could happen right there on their ranch. A shudder of fear rolled through her, and she hastened her step, knowing Maria would be following with a bowl of water and some iodine.

She entered the room quietly and sat down next to Lydia. Tears streamed down Emily's face as she saw the evidence of the attack Lydia had suffered. She leaned over and brushed a strand of hair from Lydia's face.

Emily cried, "My poor child, look at what he did to you."

They embraced and cried together until Maria brought the water and iodine. The small Mexican woman left the room muttering in Spanish.

Emily carefully cleaned Lydia's lip and dotted iodine on it. Lydia winced with the sting of the medicine before she fell back against the pillow and dozed off into a fitful sleep.

Emily never left the room but moved to the little couch and prayed for her dear children.

Joseph's blood boiled close to the breaking point. "What do you mean he is gone!" he yelled.

Buck had sent Will into town for the sheriff as soon as Joseph told him what had happened and sent Shorty to retrieve Cutter from the stall. But Shorty came back empty-handed and reported there was no sign of Cutter or his horse.

Joseph's fist made contact with the stable wall, adding to the cuts and bruises from his earlier encounter. He had no one else to blame but himself. He should have made sure that Cutter was restrained before he left with Lydia, but he was so sure the man would remain unconscious that he never gave it another thought.

No one said a word as Joseph took his frustration out on several inanimate objects and stalked back to the house. Before going to the house, Joseph told Buck to inform the men that they were to be on a constant look out for Cutter. The sheriff would do what he could, but the Circle B planned on giving him a little help.

When Spencer Atwater arrived, it was evident that seeing Lydia's battered face bothered him. Joseph was sure that a decent lawman like Spencer would take pleasure in tracking down a lowdown man that would beat on a woman. The sheriff tried to be a crusty fella on the outside, but Joseph noticed he was partial to the womenfolk. Why, his insides were probably turned to mush just like Joseph's.

Spencer sat patiently as Lydia and Joseph unfolded their story, with the women wiping a few tears. He asked them a few questions and was about to leave when Joseph mentioned that Cutter had approached his mother too.

Spencer's and Lydia's heads turned with surprise, neither one knowing about the incident. Emily told about discovering Cutter in the garden and shocked even Joseph with the details she shared about the encounter.

The women hugged each other as the men shared a look of distress. Joseph's opinion of the sheriff grew when he saw how upset this news had made him, making it evident to Joseph that the sheriff had some feelings for his mother.

The men excused themselves and spoke in hushed tones outside the door. Spencer promised Joseph he would look into things on his end and admonished Joseph to keep a look out for Cutter. He warned that a man like that is hard to figure and may try to come back here for either woman.

Joseph noticed the reference to Emily and smiled his appreciation to the sheriff. He watched as the older man rode off toward town and wondered exactly what Spencer Atwater thought about his mother.

The rest of the evening was spent very quietly with a light supper and everyone retiring early. Joseph guided Lydia to their room and disappeared back into the hall while she readied for bed.

Minutes later, he found her sitting on the bed brushing her hair. He wondered why she had not fixed the board yet but never asked. Sitting down beside her, he took the brush and began stroking her hair.

When he finished, he laid the hairbrush on the dresser and watched her braid her hair. Neither spoke, but several times their eyes met and held for many moments. She smiled coyly and moved to get under the covers.

His eyebrows shot up when she never moved to get the board but patted the bed beside her.

"You're forgetting something," he gently scolded.

"No, I'm not." She winked.

A tired sigh slipped through his lips. Were they to go through this battle every night?

He reached under the bed and brought out the board.

Her face fell, and she challenged, "I thought you said you loved me?"

He raked his hair and acknowledged, "I did, but that doesn't change anything. I've told you over and over again that we can never have a real marriage. I'm sorry," he repeated, tired of having to remind her.

Tears streamed down her face, and she threw back, "No, you're not. You knew exactly what kind of a relationship I would be locked into, and you still went through with this marriage." Bitterness flowed from her lips for the first time.

Joseph felt as if she had stabbed him. What she said was true, but now there was no way he would let her out of the marriage, because he loved her. He left the room and never came back.

18

QUIETLY JOSEPH STOOD OUTSIDE THE open window of their bedroom waiting to hear Lydia's prayer. Many minutes passed, and no prayer was offered. Fear gripped his heart, and he knew that when he had stepped out of that door this evening, things had changed.

He dragged through the darkness to the bunkhouse for a bedroll and trudged back to their window. Feeling numb, he spread the roll beside the house under their window, planning to stand guard every night until Cutter was found.

He grumbled and groaned as his aching shoulder lay upon the hard ground unwilling to give like his soft bed.

This is a bed of your own making, the thought crossed his mind, accusing and convicting him at the same time. He knew the Lord had been trying to whisper to his soul, but he had stubbornly been ignoring the prodding of the Holy Spirit.

Trust Me, Joseph, My plan will work. I have brought Lydia into your life for a purpose, just trust Me.

The words of the Holy Spirit echoed deep within Joseph's heart, but he set his jaw and refused to believe that he was unable to handle the situation on his own.

Instead, he silently prayed, *Lord, I know I've made a mess of things, but I think in time, my plan will work. Lydia just needs to understand, to see why things are best this way.*

Joseph knew there should be peace in his heart, yet his heart was filled with doubts and confusion. He knew that following the

Lord should give joy, yet he was miserable. He knew that obeying the Lord was the only way for true happiness, yet he was determined to have his way.

Long into the wee hours of the morning, Joseph wrestled with his thoughts and the convicting power of the Spirit, but as sleep over took him, he still had not yielded to the Lord.

Sneaking into their room the next morning, he retrieved some work clothes, never glancing toward Lydia, missing the way she had fallen asleep on his side of the bed, hugging his pillow close to her heart.

Aching and throbbing muscles protested with each step he took toward the bunkhouse. With a day's worth of stubble covering his disgruntled face, he stepped inside and dared any man to speak to him.

Several shocked faces greeted him, but no one spoke. Never had they seen their boss in such a mood. His hair was standing on end, dark circles under bloodshot eyes testified that he had not slept, and wrinkled clothes proved that he had not enjoyed the comfort of his own bed.

Joseph shaved, changed, and left the bunkhouse without a word. He had hoped that he could sneak into the kitchen for a quick cup of coffee and a biscuit and be gone before anyone noticed, but that was not to be.

"Good morning, Joseph," came a sweet voice as soon as he crept into the kitchen.

Lydia stood alone in the room pouring a cup of coffee. She handed it to Joseph and poured one for herself. Leaning against the counter, she took a quick sip of the hot liquid and set the cup down beside her.

"I'm glad I caught you before you left," she whispered.

His aching head jerked up, wincing with the pain and wondering how she knew he planned to leave. His eyes narrowed, examining her appearance. She was just as lovely as ever. There were no telltale signs that she had endured the sleepless kind of night that he had endured.

Her blue eyes were clear, and she was fully dressed, ready for another day. It seemed the only evidence of what she had been through yesterday was an angry bruise and swollen lip, reminding him of Cutter and causing a sneer to pull at his lips.

She moved close to him and held onto his arm so she could reach up on tiptoes to kiss his cheek. She caressed that cheek and traced the black marks under his eyes. Her hands moved to his, and she gently studied the bruised, cut-up knuckles.

Moving to the cupboard, she brought down the witch hazel and carefully applied the medicine to his wounds. He stood stone-still and wondered at the kind of woman she was. He closed his eyes in agony of soul; the tenderness she showed him heaped conviction on his head.

Finishing, she replaced the bottle in the cupboard and spoke, "I'm sorry about the things I said last night."

No, I should be the one apologizing, Joseph's thoughts incriminated him.

"Joseph, I don't understand why everything has happened like it has," she admitted softly, "but I believe the Lord is in control, and He will work things out for our good."

Glistening tears gathered in Lydia's eyes, and she smiled weakly, affirming that she had spent time with the Lord too, but in a very different way.

She is trusting, why can't you? Believe the things the Lord has been speaking to your heart.

Joseph wanted to believe, but fear held him back. It was those fears that he had been holding onto for half of his life. They had formed his way of thinking and made him the man that he was today. Those fears had driven him to devise the contemptible plan that was keeping him from true happiness.

He was tired of words. Reaching around her, he grabbed a fresh biscuit and a slice of side meat. He dropped a kiss on her cheek without a word and left the house.

Joseph shoved the biscuit into his mouth, wishing he had brought his coffee with him. As he walked to the stable, he wondered why she had to be so sweet. He remembered hoping the Lord would send her to him homely and hateful, but she was quite the opposite.

Lord, why have you been working against me from the start?

Chewing his side meat, he entered Titus's stall and began to saddle him. He patted the magnificent horse and stated, "You're the only one around here that's on my side, aren't ya, boy?"

The sun was breaking over the horizon when Joseph rode out of the yard. It was breath taking to see the first rays of a new day explode across the high skies of the New Mexico Territory. The light cast patches of shadow as it hit the small scrubby bushes that dotted the hills of the Circle B.

It was the promise of a new day, but to Joseph Banister, it was the continuation of an unsettling question: What to do with Lydia?

Joseph gave Titus a nudge, and the powerful animal leapt into a gallop across the plains, quickly bringing them to the grazing herd. The long horns were feeding on the spring growth of the land, and soon the summer rains would turn the land into a lush pasture to fatten the beeves for market.

Shorty rode up beside Joseph and greeted him with a chipper good morning, to which Joseph wanted to growl, but he held himself back. There was no reason to alienate everyone!

"How's the misses?" Shorty quizzed beginning a conversation.

"Fine. Uh … she's got a mean-looking bruise and a fat lip, but she'll be fine. Appreciate you asking."

"Good, I brought Susie in this morning to spend some time with Lydia … uh … Mrs. Banister," Shorty quickly corrected himself to show his due respect.

Shorty continued, "Boss, I was wondering if you'd like to do some fishing tomorrow? I noticed they're jumping clean out of the river next to the cabin."

Joseph grinned as he pictured sitting under the shade trees and tossing a line into the water enjoying a lazy afternoon. He knew that's exactly what he needed.

"Shorty, I'd love to go fishing after church tomorrow."

"Church?" Shorty asked.

"Yes, tomorrow's Sunday, isn't it?"

"Well, yeah."

"Listen," Joseph began with a proposition, "why don't you and Susie come to church with us. Then we can eat and go fishing on a full stomach?"

"Susie mentioned something about church the other day. She said Lydia had invited her after some kind of de … devotion?"

Joseph twisted in his saddle with a puzzled look across his face, and Shorty went on to explain.

"Susie said that after lunch, Mrs. B and your wife have a time when they read the Bible and pray together. It seems that Suz joined them and was interested in the things Lydia … uh … your wife was saying."

Lydia has been reading the Bible. When was the last time you opened a Bible, Joseph? The Lord convicted his heart.

"What kind of things did Lydia say?" wondered Joseph.

Now Shorty shifted in the saddle to face Joseph. "Susie said it was something about a rock that gave some people some water?" Shorty finished lamely.

"Oh, she must have been talking about Moses," recognized Joseph. "I heard that story a long time ago."

"You believe such a thing could happen, Boss?"

"Yep." Joseph grinned at Shorty and remembered how exciting it was to learn about the power of God. "I believe in all the miracles God did through Moses."

Shorty's squinted eyes spoke of his surprise and doubt. "She said Lydia told her there was some way that a person could get their sins washed away in the water. Did she mean being baptized?"

It had been a long time since Joseph had witnessed to anyone, and he felt unworthy to attempt it now. Over the years, he had tried to talk to the men about the Lord and sometimes even saw some come to the Lord, like Buck did, but Joseph realized that it had lost its importance somehow. It scared him to consider that the Lord was not as important to him as He had once been.

"No, being baptized is different. Lydia was talking about Jesus and how He can wash our sin away."

Just then Buck galloped up and slid his horse to a stop. His tan face was pale, and Joseph felt a tightening in his gut.

"Boss, you better come look at this," he advised and galloped away.

Joseph and Shorty shared a puzzled look and swiftly turned their mounts in the direction that Buck had disappeared. Joseph slowed Titus to a walk when he saw the huddle of men ahead; Shorty did the same.

They dismounted in unbelief as they saw three dead steer in the midst of the group. Upon closer examination, it was clear to see that each had been shot several times and carved in their side was a giant, bloody *C*.

Joseph paled as he understood what it meant. "Cutter," he hissed.

Cutter was sending Joseph a message loud and clear: he was still out there, and he meant to hurt Joseph Banister!

Joseph raked stiff fingers through his hair and replaced the Stetson. His mind flew to Lydia and thoughts of her in Cutter's grip with his knife to her throat. He couldn't let it happen again. Shoving his hands hard into his pockets, he wondered how he could stop that man. Buck's voice snapped him back to the men.

"I want everyone carrying sidearms and be sure to have rifles when you're out on the range. We'll have to stay alert at all times for Cutter. He's unpredictable, and he means to hurt this ranch and the folks on it," Buck ordered, grimly reminding the men.

Shorty laid a hand on Joseph's arm. "If it's all right with you, I think I'd feel better if Susie stayed at the ranch every day until we get this guy."

Joseph nodded his agreement and mounted Titus. "Buck, you take care of things here. I'm headed home."

Shorty followed Joseph to the ranch to let Susie know she should stay there until he finished for the day and to watch his boss's back. No one knew where Cutter lurked, and it was evident he had it in for Joseph.

They found the women on the patio reading Lydia's Bible. Joseph shook his head, amazed that Lydia had been through so much and was still willing to give of herself and her God.

Conviction pierced his heart when he considered the way he had been acting. He longed to go to the rock and find some way to gain peace with the Lord, but not today and probably not until Cutter had been found and put behind bars.

Joseph hated to frighten the women, especially Lydia, but they needed to know to be cautious. Cutter was out there somewhere and may strike at any time.

The wide eyes of his wife and mother greeted him, and he could tell that they had guessed something was wrong. He told the women what he felt they needed to know of the morning's incident. Emily became very solemn, and Susie flew into her husband's arms, but Lydia stood very still, only her swollen lip quivered.

Suddenly all color drained from Lydia's face, and fearing she would faint, Joseph swept her up into his arms as he had yesterday. He carried her into the living room, leaving the others to talk on the patio.

He set her down on the couch and sat beside her. Taking her hand in his, he declared, "Lydia, tomorrow I'm taking you to town to get the train to go back to St. Louis."

Lydia's head jerked around to face him, surprise and hurt evident.

Exhaling, Joseph tried to explain, "I want to know that you are safe. That's why you're going back to your aunt's house."

She slowly shook her head.

"I won't go, Joseph," she whispered firmly. "I know that I am to be submissive to my husband, but I will never feel safe if I'm away from you."

Lord, for once, why can't she do things my *way!*

The thought came back to his mind, *I know how you feel. I have been wondering when* you *would begin to do things* My *way.*

Joseph felt overwhelmed; his world had been changed in just one week, and he felt completely powerless to change it or control it.

Lydia cupped his cheeks with her hands and gazed deeply into his eyes.

"I promise that I will do anything you tell me to do," her voice broke as tears slid down her cheeks, "but please don't send me away."

Joseph snatched her up into his arms, feeling as if he could squeeze her in two. Relief filled his soul, knowing life was not worth living without her. *Lord, please help me keep her safe.*

When Joseph was sure Lydia was all right, he took his mother aside and related all the details of the morning's incident. He asked if she would go with Rusty into town and notify the sheriff. With twinkling eyes, she jumped at the opportunity.

"But ... but ... Sheriff," the frustrated deputy stuttered to a stop.

"Browning, I'm not askin' for the moon an' the stars here. I want two things from you," Spencer explained for the third time. "I want that safe opened pronto, 'fore I blow it up with a great big"—he stretched his arms apart, exaggerating a five-foot length—"stick of dynamite."

He reached around the desk and grabbed a yellowed copy of a wanted poster and shoved it into the deputy's face. "And I want more information on this man, and I want it like yesterday!" his voice rose into a high-pitched holler.

Emily had been witnessing this display of Clayton's new sheriff for several minutes. The deputy's eyes had cut to her when she entered the office, but Spencer's back was to her, and he was quite unaware that she was present.

"I sure would like to know," she interrupted dryly, "where I could get me a stick o' dynamite like that!"

Spinning on his heel, Spencer's huge smile warmed her. Perhaps he was as happy to see her as she was to see him.

The sheriff tried in vain to control his smile as he rebutted her wise crack, "Well, well, if it isn't the woman with *all* the directions."

"Not *all* the directions, Sheriff, I'm still waiting to find out about that dynamite," she smarted off and then snapped her fingers as if remembering something. "I've got it! It must be from Texas. I heard everything is bigger in Texas!"

The deputy's chuckle snapped the sheriff's head in his direction. He quipped, "Are you still here?"

The deputy stumbled around the desk dropping the wanted poster at Emily's feet. She bent to pick it up when she gasped at the sketch of familiar, cold, dark eyes staring back at her.

Holding it up, she shuddered, "This is ..." Growing pale, she backed into a chair beside the desk.

Spencer was by her side instantly, fanning her face with all his might. He looked to his bewildered deputy and barked, "Don't stand there looking pretty, Deputy. Get this woman some water!"

The deputy jumped and quickly poured Emily a glass of water and handed it to her. After several sips of the refreshing liquid, she was able to go on.

"This is the man that was in the garden."

"What?" the sheriff shook his head. "This is Duce Dawson, part of 'Black Jack' Ketchum's Gang. It's been rumored he may have ridden with Butch Cassidy's Wild Bunch too."

Growing perturbed, Emily lifted her chin and challenged, "I can read, Spencer Atwater! But I am telling you this is Cutter, Dirk Cutter, the man that trespassed in my house, accosted my daughter-in-law; and shot up three steers, carving his initial into their sides."

"He did what?"

"Are you so old you're hard of hearing, Sheriff?" She smiled when she could not resist another jab.

Spencer smiled despite himself.

The deputy had been painfully silent until now, but his muffled guffaw brought the sheriff's stormy expression back to him. He pointed and the deputy stumbled out the door and disappeared.

Pulling up another chair, Spencer sat in front of Emily and wagged his finger. "Speaking of Cutter, what in the world are you doing in town unescorted?"

"Why, Sheriff, I believe that you care."

"Mrs. Banister, it is my job to care."

Feigning a pout, Emily played, "I bet that's what you say to all the girls," and she flirtatiously batted her lashes.

Spencer laughed with delight at her flirting and gave back, "Why, Mrs. Banister, if I didn't know better, I would say you are flirting with me."

"No, Mr. Atwater, if I were flirting with you, believe me"—she winked—"you would know it."

"I look forward to it, Mrs. Banister." He smiled a mischievous grin.

Entering the office, Rusty cleared his throat interrupting the moment the couple had shared.

"Excuse me, Mrs. B., but I wouldn't want the boss to get worried about us or something," he said, faltering at his simple admonition.

"Yes, Rusty, thank you for reminding me," she immediately became businesslike. "Now, come here please and tell me of whom this sketch reminds you."

Rusty clomped over the floorboards with his boots and examined the wanted poster Emily help up.

"Cutter," he spit out. "That is Cutter."

"All right," the sheriff admitted, "I just received the poster this morning from Phoenix. I'll have my deputy wire them and get me some more information. Now tell me about the steer."

Emily described the terrible episode of the morning, and Spencer verified its meaning with a grim face. He assured her that he would do everything within his power to round up Cutter, or whoever he was, and lock him up for good.

Emily stood to leave, but Spencer stopped her with one more question.

"Mrs. Banister, since you know directions so well, I was hoping you could direct me to a church for services tomorrow."

Her eyes twinkled with pleasure in hearing that he was a church-going man. She rested her hands on her shapely hips and beamed, "As a matter of fact, I know of a wonderful church."

She gave him directions and times for her church and ventured on to invite him to the ranch for Sunday dinner, of which he gladly accepted.

19

JOSEPH MANAGED TO SLEEP A little better and rose looking forward to going to church. He knocked softly at their bedroom door, hoping Lydia was awake. She cracked the door, a bare shoulder peeking around the wood and teasing Joseph with its creamy softness.

She asked for a minute to get her dress on, then allowed him to enter. He could hardly take his eyes off her. She had parted her hair and twisted it into a bun worn low at the back of her neck. Her dress was a soft pink with tiny white dots embroidered over it. It sported a high ruffled collar, a V-neckline with more ruffles, and a full skirt.

"Good morning, Joseph." She smiled, "I thought you might like to bathe before church this morning," she offered, waving toward the full tub of water.

He shook his head with a sigh. "Is there anything you don't think of?"

He strolled across the room and dropped a wet kiss on her cheek. "Thank you, I would like to smell better since we're going to church," he couldn't help flashing her a cheeky grin.

Lydia smiled back at him, then excused herself so he could bathe.

Joseph stepped out into the bright sunshine and was amazed to find a caravan of wagons lined up outside the stables. He walked toward the line, smiling at Buck struggling with his string tie. He offered his help and asked where the men were headed. To his surprise, Buck told him they were all going to church.

Joseph walked over to Rusty and expressed his pleasure over his decision to go to church. Rusty told Joseph he had promised Mrs. Banister. Joseph smiled and was glad to hear that his mother had been working on the young man.

Then he noticed old hard-hearted Shotgun, crutches and all, lying in the back of the wagon. Gawking at the old man, Joseph questioned him about his decision to attend church. Shotgun told Joseph he had promised Mrs. Banister. Joseph smiled again and was shocked that his mother had convinced Shotgun to accompany them to church.

At the end of the caravan, Joseph greeted the Lawsons, proud to see that Shorty had accepted his invitation. He nodded to Shorty and raised his hat to Susie, saying, "Good morning, ma'am, glad to see ya'll coming out for church."

She smiled back and replied, "Had to, I promised Mrs. Banister."

Joseph could hardly believe his ears. When had his mother had time to work on all these folks? When he saw her come out of the patio gate, he sauntered over to congratulate her, but she denied her participation and nodded toward Lydia, who was cheerfully greeting everyone.

Following his mother's nod, Joseph realized the *Mrs. Banister* that everyone had referred to was Lydia, his wife.

"Lydia?" he squealed.

Emily smiled, enjoying Joseph's astonishment.

"How ... I mean ... when did she ..." he floundered.

"You would be surprised what that little lady has been up to. She has visited Rusty and Shotgun every day since they were hurt, checking on their broken bones and carrying batches of cookies. Now with Susie and Shorty, she bought several things for the cabin with her own money and carried them a delicious-looking chocolate cake. Every day Susie has been here, Lydia has been able to witness to her, and Susie goes home and tells Shorty."

Emily paused and shook her head. "That little lady is very special, Joseph, and you have no idea how blessed you are to have her as your wife."

I wish I knew how blessed I was, Mother. He sadly admitted to himself.

When Joseph arrived back at his buggy, Buck informed Joseph that several of the men were staying around to watch over the ranch; however, they had all promised Mrs. Banister they would attend church too. They came up with a plan to rotate church attendance until things settled down.

The wagons were loaded, and Joseph helped Lydia into their buggy. On the way to church, Joseph questioned her, "I was surprised to hear that you know the men so well."

A grin tugged at the corners of her mouth. "I waited for a few days, and when you failed to introduce me, I introduced myself."

Emily spotted Spencer as soon as the Circle B caravan entered the church yard. He had transformed from a country sheriff to a Texas gentleman, and Emily liked the look very much. His eyes took in Lydia, and his exhaled sign of relief spoke of his caring heart. He said as much when he greeted the couple.

"Good morning, Joseph and Lydia." Tipping his hat to her, he complimented, "Ma'am, you are lovely enough this morning to be a Texas Belle," and he smoothly raised her hand to his lips.

Lydia blushed with such attention, while Joseph growled and was rewarded with a poke in the ribs from his wife. Joseph pulled her arm possessively closer to his side, and they continued into the church with a string of visitors behind them.

Then Spencer turned his attention to her. His eyes followed her as she approached, and he had a huge smile spread across his face.

She spoke first, "I see that you were able to follow my directions, Sheriff."

"Yes, I have a very good memory," he proudly informed her and praised her beauty too. "My, my, Mrs. Banister, you are a vision of loveliness," and he repeated his earlier action and swept her hand to his awaiting lips with an added twinkle in his blue eyes.

"But not lovely enough to be a Texas Belle, Mr. Atwater?" she quipped, sliding her hand from his, smiling coyly, and entering the church.

Emily was profoundly glad that Spencer couldn't read her mind, for at that moment, she would have preferred to be a summer bride!

Joseph introduced Lydia to members of the church family as they came by to welcome her. They received satisfied looks from older women that thought Joseph Banister should have taken a wife years ago and disappointed looks from younger women that thought he should have chosen them!

The pew filled easily with Shotgun on the far end of the pew with a chair in the aisle to prop up his broken leg, Rusty, the Lawsons, Emily, Lydia, and Joseph claiming the inside end of the pew. The sheriff found a seat directly in front of Emily much to Joseph's concern.

He rolled his eyes heavenward. *These women are running me ragged, Lord!*

After several hymns, and a special solo, Preacher Henley claimed his pulpit. He thanked the congregation for their prayers in the passing of his brother in Raton and expressed how much they appreciated all the acts of kindness shown to his family in their time of sorrow. Then he proclaimed it was good to be back at home and in their church.

He read the text from Proverbs 14:12, "There is a way which seemeth right unto a man." Then he began his message.

"The verse in Proverbs continues, but today, I want to think about just the first part of that Scripture. We like to do things our own way, don't we? From changing recipes to raising a garden, we have our own way of thinking. And in some areas of life, there's no harm in creating new and better things, but in the realm of spiritual things, we are to do things God's way.

"Our message this morning will show how Jesus Christ is beautifully pictured as the manna in the story of the children of Israel. We will see the Lord's way to handle the manna and what happened when the children of Israel did things the way that seemed right to them.

"The story of the children of Israel is rich with pictures of Jesus Christ. He is our Passover Lamb in Exodus 12, He is the Rock and the life-giving Water in Exodus 17, and He is the Bread of Life, the manna, in Exodus 16. I believe the picture of Jesus Christ as the Bread of Life, as He is called in John chapter 6, is my favorite, but we first see Him as the Bread here in Exodus. The Israelites had been in the wilderness for about a month when they murmured to Moses that they had no bread to eat.

"So the Lord rained bread from heaven for His children. Every morning after the dew had disappeared, a small, round wafer-like object covered the ground. The people were instructed each morning to gather a certain amount for each family member. They were not to keep it overnight but gather it fresh every morning. And on the sixth day, they were to gather twice as much, and it would keep for the next day, which was the Sabbath. Every day as the sun grew hot, the manna melted away until it reappeared the next morning.

"But there were those among the people that wanted to do things their own way. They decided to gather more than what they needed for the day, unwilling to trust that the Lord would take care of them, yet in the morning, they found the leftover manna had bred worms and stank.

"The Lord was trying to teach His people that He would supply their needs. He gave them His plan for the manna, and they only needed to believe and trust Him.

"This is an example for us today. The Lord has provided whatever we need. He has provided a way of salvation through the shed blood of His Son, but we must believe and trust in His plan. We must do it God's way.

"The Lord has provided for our physical and emotional needs too. We don't need to plan and struggle, but just believe and trust in Him. We must do things God's way."

While the preacher closed the message with an appeal for those that needed prayer, Joseph's mind repeated the words of God's man: We don't need to plan and struggle but to believe and trust.

Wasn't that what Lydia was doing? She said almost the very same thing yesterday morning: to trust the Lord would work things out. But he'd devised his own plan for working things out. Never once had he consulted with the Lord. He had been telling the Lord how it was going to work!

Lord, it's not Lydia that needs to understand, it's me*!*

Joseph's prayer had been simple but sincere: he needed to know the Lord's plan.

20

AFTER MARIA'S DELICIOUS MEAL, JOSEPH and Shorty invited the sheriff to join them fishing. Joseph sensed that Spencer would have preferred to spend the afternoon with his mother, but he agreed to the men's invitation.

They saddled up their horses and headed for the Lawson cabin to see the fish that Shorty claimed were jumping clean out of the river. After tethering the horses in the shade of the trees that lined the riverbank, they settled in for a lazy, quiet afternoon.

Joseph and Shorty pulled off their boots and socks, rolled up their pant legs, and dipped their hot feet into the cooler river water. Spencer laughed at the sight and commented that it made the big men look like young boys.

When they felt sufficiently cooled, they pulled their feet out and threw their fishing lines in. The younger men settled in for some snoozing fishing. But since the sheriff was from the east, east Texas that is, and was unaware of this kind of fishing, he started a conversation.

Heads had whirled around in unbelief as Spencer stretched his arms and declared that he thought it was a good message this morning, that it reminded him of his preacher back home.

Shorty could hardly believe that the sheriff was a churchgoer too and said as much.

Joseph feigned napping as he listened to Spencer's story. He admitted that he'd been going for many years, but that just going to church didn't mean he was a Christian. In his younger days, he thought that if he could get into a church now and again, everything was sure to be right between him and God.

When he mentioned that his wife had helped him to see that he wasn't right with God, Joseph's eyes shot open, and he started listening in earnest.

Joseph could tell that the sheriff's reminiscing took over as he told them about those early days. They had been married young yet never had much time together, he and his wife, Tess. As a new Texas ranger, he thought he could take on the whole of Texas. He chuckled when he told them how virile he'd felt.

He'd been gone more than he was at home, and when he was home, he was wishing he was gone. Tess sure had put up with a lot, but somehow she loved him and kept trying to help him. She would preach to him every chance she had, saying that she didn't want to be in heaven without him.

She wore him down; between her and the Lord, he confessed he didn't have a chance. He was under such conviction that he nearly ran to the altar to get saved. But he was ashamed to say that there were a few things in his life that he wasn't willing to put in the Lord's hand; the worst was his temper.

It still shamed him as he thought about his hot, out-of-control temper. He had treated Tess real bad sometimes. He made it plain that he never hit her, but she put up with a filthy mouth, all the time yelling, complaining, and belittling her.

A smile transformed his face when he explained that the good Lord helped him to see that behaving that way was his choice, and it was a sin. The Lord showed him that he needed to confess his sin and God would help him to tame it. And he was there to testify that the Lord did just that. Sometimes he still got riled, but he knew that if he confessed it, the Lord would forgive him and help to control it.

Spencer ended his story by telling the men that he had lost his wife and child during childbirth and never remarried.

Then Shorty asked him how he knew that he needed to be saved, and Spencer retrieved a worn Bible from his saddlebag and showed Shorty from God's Word how to be saved. When the *Amen* was said, Shorty shared that he had asked the Lord to forgive his sin and save him. And the Lord did!

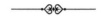

Later that evening, a buggy bounced along the bumpy path that led to a nearby rise on the west side of the ranch. The heat of the day was cooling fast, and Emily was thankful for her shawl, pulling it closer.

The sky was just beginning to color with the rays of a setting sun, as the buggy topped the rise, and the horizon could be seen in all its beauty. The evening sun began to slowly sink behind the hills to the west with bright pinks and mellow purples streaking across the high sky in front of the couple.

"Are you cold, Mrs. Banister?"

"No, not really, Sheriff," Emily sighed.

"If it's all right with you, I'd like it very much if we could be on a first-name basis." Spencer tenderly smiled as he pulled Emily's hand into the crook of his arm.

"I would like that very much, Spencer." A hint of a blush covered her face as she spoke his name.

"It's been quite a day, Emily," Spencer announced.

"Oh, it has been, that's for sure. And look at that sunset, Spencer. Have you ever seen anything so beautiful?" she asked as her gaze admired the way the sky changed as the sun lowered in the horizon.

Never taking his eyes off Emily, he replied, "No, I don't think I have ever seen anything so beautiful."

Emily sighed contentedly. "It has been a wonderful day. Have you ever heard of a husband and wife being saved on the same day, at almost the same time, but in completely different places?"

She turned to see that he had been staring, and her smile grew. He was such a pleasant man, and she enjoyed his company so much. Since the time they met, she felt like a young woman daydreaming and longing for love again.

"No," he admitted, "I can't say I've ever seen it happen that way until today. It's always a joy to lead someone to Christ. Did you hear how it happened?"

Emily patted Spencer's hand and said, "No, but I was hoping you would tell me about it."

Spencer gave Emily his story just as he had shared it with Joseph and Shorty. He recounted the way he was able to use the Bible and lead Shorty to the Lord.

Spencer's memories ended as he told Emily, "I knew I was going fishing. I just didn't know I was going fishing for men!"

She laughed with him and offered, "I'm sorry to hear about your wife. My husband died several years ago, and I understand how it feels."

Spencer was very quiet for several moments before he took Emily's free hand into his and admitted, "I had never thought I would be blessed to find love again, but I believe the Lord is showing me all things are possible."

"Oh, you old romantic fool," Emily lovingly pronounced, rewarding him with a soft kiss on his cheek.

His eyes twinkled with love, and he turned in the seat to face her. "Does that mean you would approve of an old fool like me coming to call?"

With a small gasp, Emily nodded her head just before Spencer lowered his lips to claim hers. For long moments, they sat in the buggy holding each other, delighting in the beautiful evening and their growing feelings. Emily leaned her head on his broad shoulder and vowed this day perfect.

Suddenly she snapped her head up and noted, "You never heard how Susie came to the Lord."

Spencer smiled. "No, I don't believe I had the fortune."

Emily sat back against the buggy and shared the events of her afternoon with him.

"Well, after you fellas left to go fishing, we three ladies retired to the patio with cool drinks. Lydia and I were keenly aware of Susie's contemplative mood. Lydia said she had noticed Susie's response to the message and had even seen her wipe away several tears.

"It must have been an unspoken agreement between Lydia and me to pray that poor little Susie would come to know the Lord by the day's end. Bless her heart, Lydia had been witnessing to Susie all week and continued by referring back to the morning's message.

"She was talking to me, but I knew it was for Susie's benefit. Lydia said that she had really enjoyed the message and of late had been fascinated with the story of the Israelites herself. She mentioned her study about the Passover lamb the preacher had mentioned this morning, explaining that it was one of her favorite pictures of salvation in the entire Bible.

"Of course, Lydia had Susie's attention then. I prayed with all my heart that the Lord would speak to her heart. Lydia is such a wonderful teacher, and she went on to tell the story. She said that the last plague the Lord sent to the Egyptians was the death of the firstborn. On a certain night, the death angel would fly over the land, and all the firstborn would die. But the Lord made a way of salvation for the Israelites. He told them to shed the blood of a perfect lamb and apply it to the doorposts of their house. And when the angel of death saw the blood, he would pass over the house, and all those that were under the blood would be saved.

"The people had to believe in the Word of the Lord and obey, if they wanted to be saved. And that's the way it works today. The Bible tells us that we are all sinners, and the payment of death is required. But the Lord made a way of salvation for us through His Son, Jesus Christ, who became our Lamb and shed His blood as payment for our sin. Now we only need to believe in God's Word and obey by applying that blood to our hearts through the confession of our sin and by asking Jesus to be our Savior. When our sin is covered by His blood, we are saved.

"The light of understanding began to glow in Susie's eyes, and she touched Lydia's arm with tears streaming down her face. Our little Susie was just barely able to stutter out that she knew she was a sinner and wanted to know if she could believe and be saved.

"Well, Lydia pulled Susie into her arms and told her yes, that the Lord was just waiting for her to ask Him. I know Lydia was bawling like a baby, I could hear it in her voice. And me, well, I just sat there, tears running down my face, thanking the Lord I could witness the birth of a new child into the family of God.

"Then the three of us bowed our heads to a loving heavenly Father and thanked the Lord for Susie's salvation and prayed for Shorty. Afterward Susie said that she felt as though a tremendous weight had been lifted as we cried and hugged one another."

Emily finished and patted Spencer's hand again. "It has been the sweetest day I can ever remember. Lydia has helped me to see I have not been the Christian I should have been, and I've asked the Lord to help me to be more conscious of pleasing Him in all I do."

With the twinkling of the first evening star, Spencer turned the buggy around and headed toward the ranch house. The night was growing cooler by the minute, and Emily scooted closer to her Spencer.

Suddenly gunfire cracked over the top of the buggy and spooked the horses into a trot. Another shot sailed overhead, and the frightened team took off at breakneck speed, throwing the passengers hard into the back of the vehicle. Spencer lost the reins of the horses, and they were left at the mercy of the wild team.

21

LATE SUNDAY AFTERNOON EVERYONE WAS still rejoicing over the salvation of the Lawsons, except Joseph. It wasn't that he was unhappy that the couple had come to the Lord, but he inwardly fretted about his situation. For days he had been slighting the gentle prompting of the Spirit, but Spencer's words ripped away the little peace he had possessed.

While his mother and Spencer were out for a buggy ride and Lydia entertained the Lawsons, Joseph slipped away in hopes of finding some answers. He stepped into the quiet of their room and searched about until he found Lydia's Bible. He eased himself across the bed and opened the book to Lydia's first marker found in Deuteronomy 32. His eyes scanned the pages where he noted several underlined verses.

A star beside verse 18 drew his attention, and he read, "Of the Rock that begat thee thou art unmindful, and hast forgotten God that formed thee."

Suddenly it was as if the Bible had become a mirror, and he was seeing himself for the first time in a long, long time. The verse described him! He could not remember the last time he had taken time to pray. Oh, he had been to the rock to keep the Lord updated on his plans, but he had not been to the *rock*, Jesus Christ, to ask for His will to be done. He never stopped to read or meditate upon the Word anymore, even his church attendance had become sporadic.

Quickly his eyes returned to the pages of Scripture, and he found a second verse much like the first. Lydia had marked just the last phrase that read: "and lightly esteemed the Rock of his salvation." Joseph faced the truth that he had forgotten his Savior.

The admission brought hot tears streaming down his cheeks. Tears never came easy to him, but his heart was broken as he slipped from the bed and knelt in prayer. He knew that he had stopped trying to live a life that was pleasing to the Lord and returned to a life of pleasing himself.

Joseph confessed this sin and poured out his shortcomings and fears, asking the Lord to forgive him and return the joy of his salvation. The peace that Joseph had longed for flooded his soul, and he stayed on his knees for many moments, delighting in the presence of the Lord.

He swiped his big hand over his wet face and returned to the bed, again picking up the open Bible. His mind flew to Lydia, longing to share his discovery with her, but decided to wait until they were alone.

As he turned his eyes back to the Bible, another underlined verse caught his attention. He whispered a prayer that the Lord would help him understand and learn how to really give his life back to Jesus. In verse four of Deuteronomy 32, Joseph read: "He is the Rock, his work is perfect." Laying the book on the bed in astonishment, Joseph never finished reading the verse.

He stared across the room, his mind swiftly reviewing the words of the verse. For so long, he had been struggling with this plan and that plan trying to make things right in his life, but this verse referred to the Lord's work.

Joseph's plan had been a terrible failure. Did the Lord have a plan for him? Did the Lord really care enough about Joseph Banister to have a plan for his life? Could he trust the Lord to guide his life and not resort to any more ridiculous plans of his own?

Lydia is part of My *plan for you, Joseph. I brought her into your life, just trust* Me.

The words were so plain it was as if the Lord had spoken them aloud instead of whispering them to his soul. Joseph squinted one eye and wondered if he could follow the Lord's leading.

"What about the curse I bear, Lord?" he pleaded. "Was Spencer right about the things he said about his temper? Is this a choice that a man makes or is it something that is out of my control?"

He loved Lydia and longed to be a real husband to her, but until he knew the answers to those questions, he would leave things as they were.

A loud commotion coming from the patio interrupted his thoughts, and he left the room to investigate. By the time he made his way onto the patio, a small crowd had gathered around his very distraught mother.

"It was him. I know it was," she cried hysterically. "He tried to kill us, Spencer. He tried to kill us."

Joseph shoved his way through to his mother, kneeling beside her and taking in her pale, pinched face.

"What happened? Who was trying to kill you?" Joseph questioned anxiously.

Emily turned fearful eyes to her son and whispered, "Cutter. He's back. No, no, Joseph, he never left," and she dissolved into tears.

Joseph stomped across the patio, Lydia close behind him as he entered their room and fastened his gun belt to his waist.

"Joseph," she cried, fear written on her face, "what are you doing?"

Staring off into the distance, he finished buckling his belt and shoved his gun into the holster. He glanced down at Lydia and rasped, "I'm tired of Cutter and the fear he has brought to the ones I love."

He pushed her aside and marched to the wardrobe, reaching in and coming out with a rifle.

Lydia laid her hand on his arm, begging, "Please Joseph, let the sheriff handle this," tears spilling onto her cheeks.

He growled, "Who do you think Cutter was shooting at out there?" He raked his hand impatiently through his hair. "I'm going after him myself, before he kills someone."

Joseph retraced his steps through to the patio and made long strides to the gate, ignoring Lydia's protests.

Spencer and Shorty raced out in front of Joseph and created a wall with their stance, stopping him.

"Step aside," Joseph ordered with cold, dark eyes. "I don't want to hurt you."

"Joseph, I know you're upset," Spencer tried to reason.

"No, Spencer, I was upset when Cutter trespassed onto this patio and accosted my mother," he shouted. "But after he has assaulted my wife and threatened her life and now Mother's, I'm getting even," he yelled, the veins popping out in his neck.

He had never been so angry; his face was bloodred and his hands were shaking uncontrollably. The glare that covered his eyes was murderous.

With lightning speed, Spencer drew his pistol and shoved it into Joseph's chest. The women gasped as they watched Spencer tap it hard against that bulging chest, backing the younger man up with each strike.

"Joseph Banister, I will use this on you, but only if you leave me no choice," the sheriff warned. "We are going to do this according to the law, do you understand?"

Spencer stopped, holstered his gun, and softened as he spoke again to Joseph, "Now, son, I know this is frustrating, but we can't lose our heads. When we do, we'll make deadly mistakes."

Lydia moved close to Joseph and hugged his arm. "Please, Joseph, listen to Spencer. He knows how to do these kinds of things."

Emily moved quietly to the other side of him, touching his other arm. "She's right, son, we need to think this through."

Emily turned to Spencer and offered, "Would you consider staying the night? I'm not sure it would be safe for you to travel into town."

Joseph could hardly believe Spencer had drawn his gun on him, but he knew the man had to get his attention before he did something foolish. Knowing Spencer knew what he was talking about, he admitted it when he spoke.

"Please, Spencer," Joseph murmured, "maybe we can figure out what we need to do to get Cutter, once and for all."

Arrangements were made for the Lawsons to stay in the guest room, and the sheriff took the living room couch. The three men agreed that they would go out in the morning and see if they could track down Cutter.

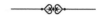

Lydia retired to the bedroom alone with a heavy heart. It had been such an emotional day filled with tears of joy and fear. That seemed to describe all her days here at the Circle B. One moment she felt as if happiness had been obtained only to have it snatched away again.

She was surprised to see her Bible open on the bed. Sitting down beside it, she discovered the bed covers were damp. Had Joseph been here praying? Not for the first time today, her emotions lifted, and the thought crossed her mind that perhaps the Lord had been dealing with him, and soon she would have a true marriage.

Hurrying out of her dress, she grabbed her nightgown when she heard a light tap at the door and her name whispered so faintly she almost missed it. She held her gown to her chest when the door opened, and Joseph appeared.

Her shocked blue eyes gave way to a full blush when she realized her gown was only draped in front of her.

Noticing the gown, Joseph blushed totally flustered and turned quickly, running his hand nervously through his hair.

"I'm sorry to … uh … just barge in like this," stammering with embarrassment.

Shrugging into her nightgown quickly, she offered, "No, I'm glad you came."

Surprised he peeked around to see that she was dressed. "I was hoping, I mean … uh … I know you pray before," rattling on he shoved his hands into his pockets in frustration. "Lydia, I was hoping I could … that is … I would like to pray with you."

The thick shock of hair fell across his brow as his eyes silently pleaded with Lydia. She had seen this bashful look before, and it gripped her heart every time. It seemed so contrary for such a big man who worked on having things under control.

A smile tugged at her lips, and she nodded, hoping that fresh tears would not begin to fall. Her heart raced as they knelt together beside the bed for the first time. He took her hand in his as he began to pray, the simple gesture touching her heart deeply and starting her tears.

Beginning by thanking the Lord for His forgiveness and long-suffering, Joseph prayed for family and friends, wisdom and understanding, and the safety of his loved ones. He begged the Lord to intervene in the capture of Cutter and ended his prayer with the confession that he did not know what to do concerning Lydia.

She was overwhelmed with his sincerity and honesty, but her own prayer remained the same and ended with her request that the Lord make her the kind of wife she should be and to bless their marriage.

Awkward moments followed as the couple stood facing each other, Lydia hoping he would stay and Joseph wishing he could, but too many unanswered questions stood between them and would not permit it.

He found his bedroll and moved toward the door when Lydia's plea stopped him, "Please, hold me, Joseph."

He turned to see her blue eyes clouded with fear, and when he opened his mouth to explain why he couldn't, she stopped him with a quivering confession.

"He's out there, Joseph, and you're going to leave me alone." Her voice was filled with the fear her eyes revealed.

He dropped the blanket on the floor and rushed to her, crushing her to his chest.

"I want to stay," he whispered into her hair.

She pulled away from him to see if it were true. Her eyes scanned his handsome face, and she saw his sincerity, but when she smiled with delight, he shook his head.

His hands cupped her cheeks, and his thumbs tenderly brushed them as he admitted, "I can't, Lydia, not yet. The Lord has been dealing with me and helped me to see some things this afternoon, but there are still issues that I have to resolve."

155

"Joseph, if we could just talk about it, maybe I could—"

He interrupted, "No," he growled, then softened as he gathered her back into his arms. "I'm sorry, but please trust me while I try to get some answers."

He kissed her longingly, picked up his bedroll, and left the room.

After a few hours of fitful sleep, Joseph woke with a heavy heart. He took some time to pray and asked the Lord to help in the search for Cutter, knowing that he must deal with him first. He confessed his love for Lydia and the desire to have a real marriage, but the fear that he would hurt her just like his father had hurt his mother and that he would pass this curse on to his son was ever present.

The fear was real to Joseph, and he felt as if he would strangle with it. He never thought he could love the way he loved Lydia, but he would deny himself that love before he hurt her.

He quietly snatched clean clothes from their room and freshened up in the bunkhouse. As he walked back to the kitchen, his eyes scanned the landscape around the ranch, wondering if Cutter was watching him that very moment. He shoved his hands hard into his pockets with the frustration of it all and went toward the kitchen.

One by one everyone gathered in the dining room. Over breakfast, Spencer reminded them about the wanted poster and said he would have to go into town later to see if any information had come in about it.

After breakfast, Joseph, Shorty, and Spencer headed out on horseback to try to pick up Cutter's tracks. While they were gone, the women prayed the men would be kept safe and be able to track Cutter down.

Little did anyone know that Cutter shadowed the three riders as they left the ranch. He followed them as they discovered his first campsite and grinned when they realized that he had been constantly moving, making tracking him almost impossible.

From a vantage point high behind the ranch, Cutter watched the riders stable their horses and enter the house. He sneered as his eyes followed Joseph Banister, and he promised himself that he would enjoy bringing him down.

Everyone had been somber during dinner, feeling the emotional strain of the past day's events. Emily retired early with Lydia and Joseph following. After a time of prayer, Joseph grabbed up his bedroll and left the room.

He threw it on the hard, dry ground, sick of calling the spot his bed. He dropped his large frame to the ground and sat, leaning against the house. He knew that sleep would be a long time in coming and would only grant him a few hours of rest.

When his thoughts began running in dangerous circles of long, thick black tresses and creamy soft skin, he collapsed onto the blanket and tried to gain sleep.

A strange sensation wakened Joseph later; through the darkness, he peered, wondering what had disrupted his sleep. All was quiet, but he couldn't shake the feeling that something was wrong. He jerked up into a sitting position when he realized exactly what it was: *smoke*!

22

JOSEPH SCRAMBLED TO HIS FEET and glanced toward the house. When there were no signs of a fire, he ran around the back of the patio and saw the faint glow of fire coming from the stables. He dashed to the bunkhouse, screaming fire, waking all of the hands. Men spilled out of the building pulling on pants and boots.

Joseph rushed forward to open the stable doors and free the animals. The frightened horses squealed and evaded Joseph until Rusty ran in and helped chase them out of the burning building and to freedom.

Outside, the men were throwing buckets of water to douse the flames while others took wet blankets and beat it out. Emily was awakened by the noise, and soon she was working alongside the men to save the building.

Buck called Joseph to the back of the stable. As Joseph rounded the back corner, he could see through the soot covering Buck's face how pale he had become. His foreman stood pointing Joseph's attention to the outside wall of the building. There, carved in the charred wood, a giant letter *C* glared at him.

"He's here!" Joseph yelled when he realized the fire had just been started when he smelled the smoke.

Panic's fingers gripped Joseph's heart as his wild eyes scanned the yard. He raced around the stable with Buck quick at his heels. When the men heard that Cutter was around, several ran to the bunkhouse for their side arms.

Joseph bolted for his mother. Grabbing her arm, he hollered, "Where is Lydia? Did she come out of the house?"

When his mother's eyes flew to the house, he knew she was still there.

Lydia sat straight up in the bed when she heard the yells of "fire." She quickly lit the lamp and went to the wardrobe to grab out her robe, but a wicked laugh split the silence of her room. Fear squeezed her heart, and her hand shook in midair as she was reaching into the wardrobe.

Her mouth went dry as she recognized that laugh and the man to which it belonged. Without a minute's hesitation, she grabbed Joseph's rifle and pulled it up as she whirled around toward the open window and Cutter.

He was framed by the window, and he laughed harder when he saw the gun in her hands. A dirty hand flew to his face and milked his chin where the beginnings of a beard could be seen. He grinned wickedly.

"What cha gonna do, girlie?" He laughed. "You gonna shoot me?"

"I will, Cutter," she promised, hoping to sound convincing.

"Maybe you will and maybe you won't, but I don't plan on sticking 'round to find out," he paused and licked his lips before he went on. "But don't you worry, I'm not too far away, and when I come back, no gun will stop me. You tell Banister that after I kill him, I'll have you all to myself!"

His vulgar laugh could be heard well after he was out of sight.

Lydia never took her eyes off the window while she backed slowly to the bed. Without lowering the heavy gun, she maneuvered herself onto the bed and up against the headboard. She pulled her knees up to her chest and propped the rifle on them, never losing sight of the window and keeping her aim on the place that Cutter had been standing.

Silently, tears trickled down her cheeks as she kept her vigil on that window. Her arms and legs began to cramp, but she refused to move, too frightened that he would return and she would be caught off guard.

When Joseph burst through the door of the bedroom, Lydia jerked the gun up and aimed it at him, thinking it was Cutter. Wild eyes saw Joseph, but a deathly grip held the gun in place. Fear fed her mind with thoughts that Cutter was there and would hurt her. Her white knuckles gripped the gun, and fear would not allow her to lower the weapon.

Joseph froze in his spot when the rifle barrel flew up into his face. Lydia sat on the bed with a terrified stillness, and he knew that she had been frightened to death. He quietly spoke her name, but she never acknowledged him. Her eyes were glossed over with terror, and her finger was on the trigger of his rifle. He knew that a sudden move could cause her to pull the trigger without being aware it was him.

"Sweetheart? Lydia?" he tried again, never moving. "It's Joseph, honey, put the gun down. It's me. I'm here now, Lydia," he spoke softly and slowly reached out to grab the barrel of the rifle.

As he touched it, her hands flew from the gun and covered her face as she wept bitterly. He propped the rifle up against the wall, then scooped her up into his strong arms.

He lowered himself onto the bed and rocked her in his lap, crying with her because he had failed to keep her safe once again.

Her arms encircled his neck as she cried, "He was here, Joseph, right here."

"Shhh, I know, honey, but he's gone now," he tried to assure her.

"No, he's not!" she screamed as she pulled away from him, but he held her tight in his arms.

"He's here! He stood right there at that window and watched me," she cried, shivering with fear. "He said he would be back, and he was going to kill you and take me for himself."

She grabbed handfuls of Joseph's filthy shirt and glared at him with wild, fearful eyes. "Please, don't let him take me, Joseph, please!" she screamed and fell exhausted into his chest.

"No, sweetheart, I won't," he said, promising with all his heart. "You're safe." He kissed her hair and smoothed it with dirty hands, rocking and holding her until she fell into an exhausted sleep.

He lifted her up and placed her under the covers, glancing in the direction of the open window. The blood drained from his face as he thought that if Cutter had stood at that window, he would have been standing on top of Joseph's bedroll.

Heavy feet carried Joseph outside. There under the bedroom window, he found his bedroll shredded into pieces and another letter *C* carved into the wall of the house.

Gathering up the pieces that once were his bedroll, he brought them into their bedroom and hid them away. He was sure that Cutter knew he had been sleeping there and not in the room with Lydia. Not even Lydia herself had been aware of the fact that he had been so close and keeping guard over her.

But now that Cutter knew, Joseph would have to stay inside the room with her. In fact, he would not let her out of his sight ever again.

After Joseph left for the house, several flames came to life, and neither Emily nor Buck was able to check on him. Through the pre-dawn hours, Emily and the men worked to save the stables. Sooty, wet, and tired, they were finally able to declare success at the break of a new day. Buck divided the men, allowing some to rest while others kept working. He sent word to the sheriff of the night's happenings and was told that the sheriff would be out midmorning with some information of his own.

Emily was free to trudge to the house and look in on Joseph and Lydia.

She cracked their bedroom door to find Joseph fully clothed and filthy lying on top of the bed covers holding Lydia in his arms, her black braid across his chest. She would get their story later; first, she would clean up, then get some sleep.

The men of the Circle B dragged through their morning chores and were happy to see Shorty come in, refreshed and ready to work. He took the place of several tired cowpokes and was filled in on the story of the fire.

Horses were calmed and fed in the corral and the messy job of cleaning up began. Charred boards were pulled away while others passed scrutinizing eyes and were left alone. A pile of black, smelly wood began to form as piece by piece the stables were cleared and readied for rebuilding.

Later in the morning, Joseph was the first to stir, but he hated to bother Lydia whom he found draped over him. He sat for long moments praying and trying to devise a strategy to catch Cutter. He moved more than he realized, causing Lydia to jump with a squeal.

He brought her close to his chest and assured her she was safe. His heartbeat sped up a little as she nestled against his chest. His arms possessively hugged her to him, and neither wanted to move until Lydia's sniffing became loud and exaggerated. A smile pulled at the corners of his mouth as he waited for her wisecrack.

Placing her hands on his chest, she pulled herself up until she was inches away from his face. She sniffed several more times, getting closer and closer to him.

Wrinkling her nose and squinting her eyes, she teased, "It's you! I thought a skunk had entered our room."

In a flash, he was out of the bed holding her in his arms as she giggled and thrashed about.

"A skunk, huh," he countered, throwing her on the bed and pinning her down with his hands. "I want you to know that you, Missy, smell just as bad as I do."

She gasped playfully and tried to pull free, but he held her arms tight over her head, straddling her tiny body with his legs.

"Well," she sighed sarcastically, "at least I am not so dirty."

A twinkle in his eye warned her that she had said the wrong thing, but by then, it was too late. He caught both her arms in one of his hands, allowing the free arm to dust her with soot and rubbing his filthy clothes over her cotton gown.

She laughed, wildly crying for him to stop, and when he did, his dancing brown eyes gently studied her face as a lovely pink blush covered it. His eyes stopped at her lips, and he smiled just before he bent low to claim them.

A knock at the door broke the passion of the moment, but not the memory that would remain in their minds for some time. It was the sporting of a husband with his wife, and no amount of fear or doubts could change the fact that Joseph Banister had fallen deeply in love with his wife.

The voice of Maria floated under the door and called the young couple to breakfast. They passed a look of guilt between them as if they had been caught doing something improper. Lydia giggled quietly as Joseph raked a hand through his filthy hair, a sure sign that he was flustered.

The morning flew by in a rush as Joseph dogged Lydia's every step. Where he had become her shadow, Shorty was still Joseph's shadow. The ranch hand appointed himself their bodyguard and moved around the ranch house and yard within feet of them. Soon it was a foursome as Susie joined Shorty, creating a weird parade of sorts. Joseph assured Shorty that it was completely unnecessary for him to tag along, just as Lydia had told Joseph, but in the end, nothing changed, and the little parade continued to move around.

The sheriff arrived shortly after lunch and greeted the foursome and a sleepy Emily, who had just emerged from her room cleaner but still bone weary. He informed the group that word had arrived from Phoenix that most of Black Jack Ketchum's gang had been caught, and they verified that Dirk Cutter, alias Duce Dawson, had left the gang weeks before.

The sheriff also mentioned that he thought the injuries to Rusty and Shotgun had probably been the workings of Cutter. Then Joseph began to fill Spencer in on the fire and Cutter's appearance to Lydia; however, he failed to mention the bedroll he had hidden away.

After some thoughtful consideration, the men decided the only place for Cutter to have full view of the ranch, especially the back, was from a rise to the west not far from where Emily and the sheriff had been for their buggy ride.

Spencer Atwater crossed his arms over his chest and smiled at the group. An idea had popped into his head, and with the Lord's help, it just might be the thing to catch Cutter by nightfall.

After hearing the plan, Joseph made one revision, and the plan was thrown into action, each person on the ranch being discreetly informed and following precise directions.

Several cowpokes rode out in the direction of the herd, making sure one of the men was Buck Hanson. Not one man was left in the yard or outside the bunkhouse. The three women hung clothes at the line and entered the patio through the yard gate. Joseph and the sheriff left on horseback headed for town.

Watching from his vantage point, Cutter sneered with pleasure. He peered through his eyeglass at the ranch below and noted the three women lounging on the patio and Joseph riding off with the sheriff.

He was sick of this ranch and Joseph Banister. Why not just snatch the woman and be gone? Surely he had hurt Banister enough, and taking his woman would be the final blow.

Cutter gathered his things and stowed his gear, planning to ride hard and fast but never returning to the Circle B again. He walked his horse down the rise, careful not to stir the dust, and tethered his mount to a bush just behind the ranch house.

He stayed out of sight for long moments eying every building, and when he was satisfied that no one was around, he crept to the patio gate. Peering through the wrought iron gate, he placed the women in the far corner at the small table.

He could hear Lydia's soft voice and locked his eyes on his prize as he slithered through the open gate and onto the patio. Never taking his eyes off the women, he knew the moment he had been spotted.

He stood to his full height, lustfully staring at Lydia as he moved closer to the group. He enjoyed the fear in their eyes and felt his heart quicken with each step.

"Cutter!" Emily gasped her hand, flying to her throat. "I never thought you would be stupid enough to come back here in the daylight."

"Shut up, woman," he barked. "I had enough of you the last time. I've come for Lydia, but if you make me mad, you'll be sorry you did."

Emily tucked Lydia behind her, and Susie joined Emily, blocking Lydia from Cutter's view.

He crept closer and closer, nervously glancing around. He drew out his pistol and swung it back and forth, mocking.

"Aw, that's real sweet hiding my lady like that, but I'll just shoot you both, take her, and leave you dead."

The outlaw reared his head back, laughing, then snapped his pistol under Emily's chin and countered, "You are one gutsy woman." He smiled a filthy grin and lowered the gun as his dirty finger took its place and ran up her cheek. "If I weren't so hungry for Lydia, I might have settled for you."

His wicked laughter filled the air, and the women visibly quivered with fear. Lydia cried behind Emily and gripped the older woman's arm.

Cutter holstered his gun and then using both hands shoved the two women aside to reach for Lydia. His eyes brightened with lust as he touched her arm and continued up her arm to her face.

"I have burned with the desire to have you, Lydia," he whispered. "In time, you will learn to want me too."

"What about me, Cutter?" Joseph jumped out from the bushes that were behind Lydia, smashing a shotgun into Cutter's face.

The outlaw closed his eyes and shook his head slightly, knowing he had made the fateful mistake of allowing his feelings to control him. He cursed, admitting to himself that his lust for Lydia had been his undoing.

Joseph pulled Lydia protectively around him and began to explain that Shorty had dressed in some of Joseph's clothes and rode out on his horse with the sheriff, all the time hoping to lure Cutter to the house.

The sheriff and Shorty came through the gate of the patio just then and the sheriff handcuffed Cutter, congratulating him on his stupidity and promising that he would be behind bars for a very long time.

23

Buck and several deputies arrived as the handcuffs were clamped on Cutter's wrists. Joseph and Shorty followed the sheriff and his prisoner to a waiting wagon, which was escorted into town by several Circle B men.

Joseph had hoped to have a few minutes to speak with Spencer, but he felt it more important to get Cutter to the jail. There was always tomorrow; besides, Joseph knew anytime he needed to talk to Spencer, he would be there for him.

For so long, Joseph had lived with the dreadful knowledge of this curse. Because of the shame, he had never approached his mother or anyone about his beliefs and found it hard to speak of it even now. He yearned to find that it was something that he could control, yet fear continually filled his heart, feeling that he would learn, once and for all, that what he had believed as a young boy would be the truth. He would have to suffer with the knowledge that he loved Lydia but could never have her for his own.

After the wagon left, Joseph took several moments to really look at the damage to the stables. They would need to get it rebuilt before the summer rains began. It would be good to get back to work again; staying close to home had made him stir crazy.

Or was it a certain little lady that was making him feel that way?

Joseph knew he should go check on Lydia, but he also knew that he had come so close to caving in. Smiling, he shook his head, admitting she had become a definite distraction, and he needed to get a hold of himself.

Unable to cope with Lydia and his feelings, he saddled Titus and headed for the range. It felt good to give Titus his head and allow the powerful horse to gallop across the hills of the Circle B, the wind whipping water from his eyes.

Joseph, why are you running away? My work is perfect, and it involves Lydia. I am working all this for your good, trust Me.

The Lord dealt with Joseph in this fashion even as his horse took him farther and farther away. He checked the herd and wandered the fence line until the sun began to sink. Then he slowly turned toward home with a set jaw and the determination to do what was right: to follow through with *his* plan.

Lydia's eyes followed Joseph around the patio, hoping to meet his gaze, but he never looked in her direction. She was so confused by his actions. He had been so sweet this morning, remembering the sound of his steady heartbeat and wondering when the Lord would make her the beat of his heart. After Joseph's attention last night, she had promised herself that she would work on trifling with her husband's desires. But now Joseph seemed to avoid her.

Emily and then Susie hugged her and checked to make sure she was all right. Spencer nodded toward her at one point, and she returned a weak smile. Shorty patted her on the back, declaring she was quite a gal, but Joseph, her husband, did not see to her well-being.

If anyone noticed that Joseph had not returned to check on her, no one said a word; although Lydia was painfully aware of the pitiful glances that were passed between Emily and Spencer and Susie and Shorty.

Joseph had followed Spencer out, and she expected him to come back as soon as the wagon left. Shorty came back, but Joseph never did. With all this behind them, she firmly expected things would be different. Joseph had confessed his love and made things right with the Lord. What more did he need?

Lydia massaged throbbing temples and excused herself. Emily followed her and suggested a nice hot bath to ease the tensions of the past several days, and with a small amount of coaxing, Lydia went to the kitchen for a cup of tea while Carlos fixed her bath.

Susie and Shorty spoke to Emily and headed for their little cabin, relieved that Cutter was gone and things could settle down into a routine for everyone.

Emily pampered and fussed over Lydia, all of the time thinking of the things she would say to Joseph. She would pin him down, letting him know how sorry he had behaved this evening and that he had better make it up to sweet Lydia in a big way or he would have to reckon with her!

But Emily's opportunity to set Joseph straight never came, because Spencer Atwater did! Shortly past sundown Spencer pulled into the yard of the Circle B in a rented buggy with a bouquet of spring flowers.

Surprised to see him, Emily greeted him at the door with a curious smile.

"Emily, I know it's been a hard day, but I couldn't rest tonight without knowing you were all right," Spencer boldly admitted as he handed her the brightly colored flowers.

With a giddy laugh, she accepted his gift. "My, my, Spencer, you are the romantic."

"Could I offer you a buggy ride, minus the gunfire?" he jested, offering his arm.

The couple dissolved into laughter as she grabbed up her shawl, left word with Lydia, and made their way to the buggy. The evening was cool, which justified a small amount of snuggling, and it was relaxing, a welcome change from the day's stressful activities.

They spoke of Cutter briefly so as not to spoil the ride, and Emily shared her concern over Joseph's odd behavior. Spencer confessed it had bothered him too and offered a word of prayer for Joseph, which melted Emily's heart.

Spencer took Emily's hand in his and cleared his throat.

"Emily, I really came here tonight," he paused nervously and caressed her hand gently before he went on. "I came here because, well, today when I knew you would be between Cutter and Lydia," he stopped again, and the moonlight glistened off his moist eyes.

Emily swallowed several times as her heart began to flutter. When their eyes met, she knew what he would say, and ripples of delight chilled her arm and added to her excitement.

"Emily, what I'm trying to say is that I knew you were in danger, and I feared something would happen to you before I could tell you that I love you."

"Oh, Spencer," she cried and hugged his neck.

"Well now, I know this is quick and all, but the way I see it is that me and you are not spring chickens anymore. If we know what we want and we're sure that it's pleasing to the Lord, why not go for it?"

Emily was so taken with Spencer's tenderness she couldn't speak. He was so different from Richard, much more like the man that would fill a woman's dreams.

Spencer felt a warm, damp spot on his shirt and guessed, "Emily, are you crying?"

She pulled away and dabbed her eyes. "Yes, you romantic old fool," she laughed through her tears. "I thought I was helping my son to find true love, and here the Lord brought it to me."

"Does that mean"—he looked at her with hopeful eyes—"you agree with me?"

She flashed him a teary smile and cupped his cheeks with her hands. Staring directly into his eyes, she teased, "Yes, you old rooster, but I'll not marry you until you ask me proper like."

But poor old Spencer never had a chance, for Emily Banister kissed him with all the promise and passion of a spring chicken!

When Lydia entered her room, she glanced toward the window in fear of seeing Cutter's face staring back at her. She told herself she was being foolish, that he was safely behind bars in town, but she still closed the window and its curtain and fetched Joseph's gun, laying it beside the tub.

Lydia soaked in the hot bubble bath until the water had cooled, fretting over Joseph's disappearance until she had worked herself into a real snit. Why did he leave without checking on her? She was tired of his mood swings, lovey-dovey one minute and standoffish the next, sure that she would lose her mind if she had to go through life like this.

Why had the Lord brought her to this wilderness and forsaken her? She knew He had foreseen the kind of marriage she would have with Joseph. Why would He doom her to such a fate? Didn't He care for her anymore?

Lydia's thoughts ran in this course throughout her bath and while she dressed. As she stood in front of the mirror to begin brushing her wet hair, her reflection in the mirror stopped her. A new thought crossed her mind and accused her of sounding like the Israelites when they became disgruntled with God's care of them in the wilderness.

For long moments, she stared at herself, knowing that no matter what the circumstances in her life, the Lord loved her and stood beside her. Hot tears of repentance poured from her eyes as she made her way stumbling to the bedside.

There on her knees she asked the Lord to forgive her for the way her thoughts had accused Him and for her lack of faith. Lydia opened her heart to the Lord and shared her feelings about Joseph and their marriage. Once again, a sweet peace filled her heart and turned her to the Word for encouragement and instruction.

Although the room was stuffy, she would not reopen the window; and when she moved to the couch to study her Bible, the gun was always within reach. Passage after passage she read trying to find some wisdom about anger and wrath, hoping to show Joseph that those things were common to all men, but that the Lord would help him to control them.

She remembered her preacher in St. Louis teaching about things that a Christian should put off and put on. At last she found the Scriptures in Ephesians 4:22–32 and Colossians 3:8–17 and underlined them, putting stars next to the verses that said to put off anger and wrath.

Hardly able to keep her eyes open any longer, she left the Bible on the couch, promising to continue her study in the morning. She turned the lamp on the table down low. Grabbing up the gun, she headed for bed.

Only minutes later Joseph cracked the door and saw her fast asleep, the board in place dividing the bed and his gun propped up against the bedside table.

When he entered the room, he noticed how warm it was and glanced to the window, which was closed tight and had the curtain drawn. His head whipped back around to the bed and the gun beside Lydia. He would have rather faced Cutter all over again than to realize that she had been here alone and afraid.

He trudged to the couch, throwing his Stetson on the chair and raking his hand through his hair. He had failed her once again. Lowering himself to the couch, he almost sat on top of her open Bible.

She had been reading the Word probably for comfort. *Comfort you should have given her.* A great sigh raised his chest as his eyes scanned the pages that Lydia had been reading. Once again several underlined passages caught his eye.

He read the verses in Ephesians 4 and glanced toward Lydia when he understood she had been studying anger and wrath. His eyes fell back to the Scripture and verses 31 and 32: "Let all bitterness, and wrath, and anger, and clamor, and evil speaking, be put away from you, with all malice: And be ye kind one to another, tenderhearted, forgiving one another, even as God for Christ's sake hath forgiven you."

Joseph focused his eyes at a point across the room, trying to comprehend what he had just read. *Was the Scripture saying that anger and wrath was something that one could control? That one had a choice not to have an ill-temper? That it was not a trait that a father passed on to his son?*

The thoughts were overwhelming. There had been an odd sense of security in knowing and accepting the curse that he had inherited. His whole adult life had been formed by this knowledge, but now he felt that everything he had known was disappearing.

Lydia shifted in the bed and drew his attention. She was such a special young woman; under any other circumstances, he would have given his love to her without reservation. But how could he love her and treat her as poorly as his father had treated his mother?

How do you know *you will treat her that way? Besides being frustrated because of this plan of yours, have you ever mistreated her?*

Once again the battle raged in his mind. He pushed it back in some dark corner and decided to go to bed. He closed Lydia's Bible and noticed a marker hanging too far out. Reopening the book to the marked page to safely arrange the marker, Joseph found more underlined verses.

His mind said to forget it and go to bed, but his heart urged him to read them. Colossians 3 mentioned this putting on and putting off concept also, again implying that Joseph could choose whether his temper would control him or he control his temper.

He secured the book marker and snapped the Bible closed. His eyes narrowed to the little thing that slept in his bed, and he knew he must find the answers.

He shed his clothes and lowered himself into his side of the bed with the determination that he would find time in the morning to speak to his mother.

24

JOSEPH COWARDLY LEFT THE HOUSE before Lydia or his mother woke. He headed to the range with plans to check the herd, run the fence line, and anything else he could think of to keep him away from home.

Much to his dismay, Joseph's mind constantly mulled over the Scripture verses he had read. This battle that his mind waged caused him to be ill-tempered. The very thing he was trying to understand once again took control of him. His men gave him a wide berth when they recognized his dark mood.

When Lydia awoke, she was not surprised to find Joseph had been there and was already gone, probably for the day. She prayed before her feet ever hit the floor that the Lord would give her grace and wisdom for the days ahead, but she felt a certain sadness settle in her soul.

It was still early by the time she had dressed, so she settled on the couch to take up her studies. She mused over her closed Bible and prayed that her husband had read the verses that she had marked as he had done before. However, she was afraid to claim this as a sign that the Lord was working with him.

Later she met Emily for breakfast and was not too surprised to find a wonderful twinkle in her eye, feeling sure that the older woman had found something special with Spencer Atwater. Suddenly a thought crossed her mind, *If Emily and Spencer marry, there will be no need for Joseph to try to make his mother happy.* Fear gripped her heart, and she was unwilling to even think what that would mean for her marriage.

Putting the thoughts into the far recesses of her mind, she concentrated on Emily's description of the night before. Lydia was genuinely happy that Emily had found love with Spencer. Joseph's mother deserved to be happy and know the tender love that radiated from Spencer each time they were together.

For Lydia, the older woman had been a godsend, bathing her in a mother's love and allowing her to feel cherished; something she had missed from her own mother. She could understand why Joseph would deny himself happiness to assure happiness for his mother. But didn't he realize that Emily's happiness was also dependent upon his happiness. It was a vicious circle that mother and son had entered into, and Lydia found herself caught in the middle.

She could only pray that Joseph would be willing to share with his mother his fears about his father and this assumed curse that he allowed to shape his life. Since Lydia had talked to Emily, she was sure that Joseph would learn that he had misunderstood as a young boy and discover that he needed to turn to the Lord for understanding and not to lean on his own understanding.

After breakfast, Emily went into town, but Lydia wandered around the yard, visited with Rusty and Shotgun, then took the buggy to the Lawsons. She needed the distraction and the fellowship she had developed with Susie. The afternoon turned to evening, and Susie invited Lydia to stay for supper, which she gladly accepted to avoid going home.

The sun was dipping into the horizon when Joseph rode Titus into the yard and handed the care of the horse to Juan. He was keenly disappointed when Lydia was not waiting in the doorway to greet him. There was no warm smile, no soft cheek to kiss, no cool glass of lemonade, and no beautiful wife to fuss over him.

Of course, this did not help his dark mood as he stalked into the house and slumped onto the couch to pull off his boots. *Where is Lydia? She knows I come home at this time every day, and she's always waiting for me.*

He sat alone in the living room knowing that he was paying a high price for his uncaring behavior yesterday. He selfishly had hoped that she would treat him better than he had treated her, but he was learning things the hard way.

Emily strolled into the living room and would have ignored Joseph completely had he not stopped her.

"Where's Lydia?" he asked, putting on an air of innocence.

Emily's expression was one of pure shock, then it turned to smugness. "She's gone."

In seconds, Joseph had hurdled the couch and caught her by the arm before she could leave the room. "What do you mean 'gone'?" He bit back barely able to keep his control.

She smiled coolly and glared up into his face. "Joseph, you didn't expect Lydia to throw herself at you after the way you treated her yesterday, did you?"

He shoved his hands hard into his pockets knowing his mother was right but hating to admit it. He breathed deeply and looked away from her accusing eyes.

"Where is she?" he asked quietly, suddenly feeling tired.

Emily reached to her son's arm, and she told him that Lydia had taken a buggy to visit with Susie. She admitted that she had expected her home before now but thought perhaps Susie had asked her to stay for dinner.

Joseph was relieved to hear it but realized that he had a lot to think about. Emily grabbed him by the arm and pulled him back to the couch.

"Sit, Joseph," she commanded that stunned man towering over her, but he dropped himself onto the couch. "I am afraid I have let this thing go too far without saying much, but I cannot keep it to myself any longer."

Joseph's eyes followed her as she moved around the small table and pulled a chair up to face him. He knew what was coming and felt sure he deserved whatever she handed out.

"Joseph, I never thought that I could be ashamed of you, but I was yesterday," tears formed in her eyes as she spoke. "I could hardly believe that you would be so callus of your wife's feelings that you left her without a word after she had been through so much."

Emily had to pause to swipe away the tears that threatened to fall. "Son, I thought that you would be happier with a lovely wife like Lydia, that your dark moods would change, but it has become worse instead of better. From one minute to the next, we never know what will set you off. What is wrong, Joseph? Please talk to me," she ended with a plea to her son.

Joseph knew this was the opportunity that just last night he had determined to find. But instead of being honest with his mother, his mouth betrayed him. "Mother, I never asked you to find me a wife," his voice was strained.

Emily opened her mouth to defend her actions, but Joseph stopped her with a raised voice, "No, Mother, no excuses. I never wanted a wife, and when I learned you had advertised for one, I begged you to stop it." Joseph's hand raked through his hair, frustrated that he had started his talk this way.

"Joseph, why?" she asked as a tear slid down her face. "Why didn't you want to marry?"

His shaking finger brushed tears from her cheek and melted his heart. He hated that he had caused her to cry, but lately he had that effect on the women in his life.

"Mother, I … don't—" he stammered until Emily cut him off.

"Son, I've always had the feeling that you never married because of me. But I want you to understand that nothing would make me happier than to see that you and Lydia have a wonderful marriage. Joseph," she paused to get his full attention, "don't you see that my happiness has always been dependent upon your happiness. It makes me happy to know that you are happy. That's why I found a wife for you, because I believed that it would make you happy, and I still do, if you will let it."

Joseph stood, completely frustrated with the situation. All these years he had been working so hard to make his mother happy, and she had been trying to do the same for him. However in the process, they never talked to each other to find out what it would take to achieve that happiness.

He hooked his thumbs through his belt loops and began to pace, allowing the words to flow from his heart.

"I've been trying to make *you* happy, Mother. I guess we have been so busy trying to see the other happy that we never stopped to find out what it was that each of us wanted."

Joseph struggled with his words. It was so painful to share the truth with her, after all the years he had tried to keep her from it.

"I knew Father had passed the curse on to me, his son, and I did not want a wife of mine to suffer like you did."

Joseph could see that he had shocked his mother. After several minutes, her look changed to total confusion. He quickly took his seat and held her hands in his, trying to explain.

"As a young boy, I saw the way Grandfather treated Grandma. Then Father began to treat you the same way. Finally it dawned on me that Father had inherited it from his father, and that I was doomed to have the same curse."

"Joseph, I'm not sure I understand what you mean by 'curse'?"

Joseph knew he was not explaining himself very well and tried again, "Mother, I know that I have inherited Father's wicked temper, and I'm doomed to mistreat my wife as he mistreated you. That's why I never wanted to marry because I don't believe that a man can love his wife and hurt her that way, beside the fact that I don't want to father a son that would carry the curse too."

"Joseph, there is no curse," she said emphatically. "I'm sorry to tell you that I don't believe your grandfather was ever saved and that is why he never cared about the way he treated his wife. When your father and I were first married, Richard was a kind and caring husband, always considerate of my feelings and needs, but then we moved out West and lived with his parents. Your father worshipped the very ground his father walked on and believed he was the final authority on many things, including the way a husband was to treat his wife. Our move West changed everything about our marriage."

Joseph watched his mother gaze out the window, wondering if she was reliving those days. His heart hurt for his mother and the hard life she had lived. He gave her time to wipe a few fallen tears, and she continued with her story, "Joseph, I know your father loved me and you very much. I believe he was a saved man, but he allowed his father to influence him in ways that weren't Christlike. Richard began to treat me in the uncaring way that his father treated his wife. We talked about it many times, and each time, he would be repentant of his behavior, but he never changed it."

Joseph chimed in excitedly, "That's right, Mother, it was the curse. He couldn't change it because it was something that he had inherited from his father. It was out of his control."

"No, Joseph"—she shook her head emphatically—"it is not an inherited curse. It's a choice. Your father knew that he was sinning and that the Lord was not pleased with his behavior, but, Joseph, it was a choice your father made for himself."

Joseph massaged tight neck muscles, weary of trying to understand and longing for some kind of peace in his life.

Emily touched his knee, and when he turned his eyes back to her, she begged, "Joseph, believe me when I tell you that your father struggled with this problem all our married life, but you don't have to. The Lord has saved you, and He wants you to put off your anger and put on kindness."

"That's what Lydia marked in her Bible. I guess she was hoping I would read it. Does that mean that I have a choice in all this?"

Emily smiled through her tears. "Yes, Joseph, you have a choice."

"That's what Spencer said Sunday."

"He did?" Emily asked in surprise.

"Yes, he was giving his testimony to Shorty and told about his temper and how the Lord helped him to see it was a choice that he had to make. But I couldn't believe that he was talking about the same thing that I was dealing with."

"You should talk to him, son. He'll be able to help you understand how the Lord can help you." She patted his knee and prayed he would take her advice to speak with Spencer.

"Joseph, if you never wanted to marry, why did you go through with your marriage to Lydia?"

Joseph's deep sigh spoke volumes. Could he tell his mother the extent to which he suffered? And made Lydia to suffer?

"When I learned that you had sent for her to come and marry me," he began to explain, "I conceived this plan that I would marry her but never—" Joseph stopped, not knowing how to give his mother the details. Long moments passed before Emily understood what he was having trouble saying.

"Do I understand that you married that precious woman but never intended to really make her your wife in God's eyes?"

Joseph shamefully nodded unable to face his mother's disappointment. Somehow the plan had not sounded so absurd to him, but when his mother voiced the truth, he knew how ridiculous it had been. When there was no reply, Joseph looked up to see the sadness in his mother's eyes.

"Joseph, how could you not love her?"

A frustrated hand flew through his hair, rifling it hard and testifying to Joseph's dilemma. "The problem is that I do love her," he confessed and hurried on to explain. "I tried not to and even asked the Lord to make her unlovable before she got here. But one look at her, and I knew I was in trouble. She was the most beautiful woman I had ever seen, and I was no good for days."

"Yes, I remember how awkward you were, but why didn't things get any better if you had fallen in love with Lydia?"

"Mother, I married her because I thought it would make you happy, and I withheld myself from her for fear that I would father a son cursed with the family temper."

"Oh, Joseph," Emily cried, "it seems that we Banisters have made a terrible mess of things, and poor Lydia has been in the middle of all of it." When she saw that Joseph agreed, she asked, "What are we going to do to change things?"

Joseph wished he knew how to make things right, but he feared he had hurt Lydia too deeply and wondered if she would ever forgive him and learn to love and trust him ever again.

Emily sat quietly trying to comprehend this impossible situation; then, the light came on. "Joseph, did you marry Lydia just to please me?" Her voice was full of the pain she felt.

He nodded his head and confessed, "On our wedding night, I told Lydia that I would never love her and that this pretend marriage was just to make you happy. I told her I was doing all of this because I loved you and I thought it would make you happy. I counted on the love she felt for you to make it work, but I didn't count on falling in love with her and her with me."

"You mean she confessed her love for you too?"

"Yes, several days ago. That's why I had to leave the room. I just didn't trust myself with her any more. I could not risk being with her even with the board dividing the bed."

Emily just shook her head. "I don't know what you are talking about, Joseph, and I'm quite sure that I don't want to know. It is plain to see that you and Lydia are the victims of the misconceptions of a young boy that grew to a man allowing his false beliefs to rob them of true happiness. Promise me two things, dear. First, that you will enjoy the wife with which the Lord has blessed you. Then I want you to talk to Spencer and let him help you understand about your temper."

Joseph stood to his full height and pulled his mother into his arms, promising, "Yes, Mother, I will try. Now how about feeding your hungry son?"

"Food, I believe that's all you menfolk can think about, filling your stomachs." She shook her head, laughing and looking as if a great burden had been lifted from her heart.

25

WHEN LYDIA ARRIVED HOME FROM Susie's, she saw Juan grooming Titus, which meant Joseph was home. She appreciated the time she had spent with Susie and the shoulder her friend offered. Lydia felt she had to share a few things with her friend but never betrayed Joseph's confidence.

Susie promised she would be in prayer for Lydia and invited her to come back often. It had been such a blessing to have a friend like Susie, and Lydia felt grieved at the thought she may have to leave her.

She sighed defeated, and she handed the buggy over to Carlos. She peered through the darkness and decided to go through the patio in hopes of avoiding everyone.

As she stepped into the hall, she heard Emily's voice in the direction of the living room. Moving closer, she heard Joseph's harsh words that he had never wanted a wife and had begged his mother to stop the arrangements. His words were her undoing, and she fled to their room in tears.

Oh Lord, I know that I sound like the Israelites, but I do wonder what I have done to deserve this. I love you with all my heart and Joseph too, but I guess that all of Joseph's attentions have been pretend, just as he had said in the beginning. I know now he doesn't love me and never will.

Lydia's tears fell hard and fast, and her breathing was in great gasps. She undressed, moving numbly, and climbed under the covers on her side of the board.

What will I do now? It was her last thought as she cried herself to sleep.

Joseph inhaled his food, anxious to talk to Lydia and try to straighten out the mess he had made of things. When he and his mother had finished a light meal, neither of them had heard Lydia come in. Joseph went out to the stables to check with Juan and learned that Lydia had arrived shortly after he had.

He went back into the house and let his mother know she had already come home, then moved on to the bedroom. The lamp was turned down low, and Lydia was sound asleep for the second night in a row.

He had hoped to make things right between them but had to retire knowing it would have to wait for tomorrow. He sat on the bed for a long time, watching her sleep and praying that the Lord would help him to be the kind of husband she deserved.

The next morning, Joseph sat watching as Lydia's eyes peeked open to the new day. He had purposely remained bare chested hoping to show her that things were going to be different. But the shocked look and sweet blush that covered her face told him he may be moving too fast.

"Well, I haven't seen that blush in quite a while," his voice full of mischief.

"I haven't had much to blush about lately."

She threw back the covers and stomped to the wardrobe for a change of clothes. He was by her side in a flash, but she ignored him. Nevertheless, he pressed on, "I know I have been unbearable the past few days, and I want to apologize."

Her hands snatched her dress out of the wardrobe, and Joseph noticed it was his favorite, the pink one that made her irresistible. When she didn't acknowledge him, he tried a different approach.

"I like this one," he touched the dress and caressed her cheek. "It makes your cheeks a rosy pink."

The compliment didn't get him any farther, but he was determined to get her attention. He grabbed her up in his arms with a quick sweep and carried her to the couch. She kicked and clawed, but he was a man on a mission and would not be swayed by her coolness.

He sat down, holding her tight in his lap as she pushed against him with both hands on his chest. She didn't seem to be effected by having her hands on his bare chest. But he was.

A smile tugged at his mouth, but he thought better than to show it since she was riled enough. He watched her face screw up into several ridiculous positions until she finally accepted the situation and crossed her arms over her chest in a huff.

"I talked to Mother last night," he began, but she still paid him no attention, "about my father."

Now that brought her head around quickly, and their eyes met for a short moment before she turned from him again. But he took hope when he saw the sparkle in her eyes and hurried on, "I told her what I believed about his temper, and she helped to understand a little better."

Slowly Lydia's arms fell until her hands lay in her lap, never turning or speaking, but to Joseph, it was a huge sign. He continued, "I told her about our marriage too."

Lydia jumped from his lap quickly, catching him off guard and running across the room. She spit back, "What marriage, Joseph? This is not a marriage and never will be." Tears threatening to fall at the remembrance of the words she overheard last night.

"Lydia, if you will just give me a chance," he pleaded as his long legs brought him in front of her. "Please, sweetheart, hear me out." His hands reached out to touch her, but she jumped on the bed to avoid his touch.

"No, you don't care for me, and you never did. You said so yourself, this is a pretend marriage. But I don't want to lie about it anymore!"

She stood on the bed against the headboard, and Joseph was tempted to catch her, pin her down, and kiss her soundly on the lips, but he held himself in check. He asked the Lord to help him to be patient, forgetting that tribulation worketh patience!

"All right, Lydia, I see I will have to convince you I am sincere," he conceded. Grabbing a shirt and socks, he left the room.

Lydia wasn't sure if that was a promise or a threat, but she knew that Joseph was different. Was this the real Joseph or was this part of the plan? She was so confused and tired of his games.

She wedged a chair up against the door so she could dress without interruption. As she worked on her hair, unwanted thoughts traveled through her mind. *His bare chest felt so strong against my hands. He has never been without a shirt before, why now? I must keep my distance today and by all means don't look into those dreamy eyes of his!*

With her hair braided and wound around the back of her head, she made the bed and peeped out the door for any sign of Joseph. A heavy sigh left her as she slipped into the hallway, praying he had left for the day.

Much to her disappointment, he sat with his mother in the dining room waiting to share breakfast. She paused in the doorway when she saw him and chose to ignore his eyes as they followed her into the room. Any other day she would be thrilled to see his approval of her appearance, but not today!

She glided over to Emily and dropped a kiss on her cheek, then turned to her seat. Before she was able to sit, Joseph was behind her to pull out her chair, and he whispered into her hair, "You owe me two kisses since you kissed Mother first." He flashed her a cheeky grin and dropped a kiss on top of her head.

Lydia blushed a deep red, and her eyes grew as they followed Joseph back into his seat, but it was his wink that caused her mouth to gape open.

Joseph glanced at his mother and could tell she was enjoying the difficult time Lydia was giving him. He knew it would not be easy to win her back after all he had done, but his determination was greater than anything she had to dish out!

Lydia was quiet throughout the meal, answering any questions in one-syllable words. Joseph tried his best to engage her in conversation, but she remained sober. Several times mother and son exchanged questioning glances, but neither one of them could rouse her.

When Lydia had finished her last bite, Emily spoke before she could leave, "Lydia, please change into your riding clothes."

Perfect, Mother, I'll teach her to ride today.

"I'm not interested in learning, but thank you anyway," she spoke in a hushed tone and rose from her chair to leave.

"Nonsense," Emily demanded in her take-charge way, "every rancher's wife should know how to ride."

Joseph's eye twinkled. "Absolutely right, Mother, now go on and change, and I'll teach you to ride."

Joseph's smile fell to the floor when his mother corrected him, "No, dear, Will is waiting. He will teach her to ride."

"Will?" the name was spoken simultaneously by the couple as their heads whipped around to see if Emily was sincere.

"Yes, Joseph, I said Will is going to teach her. You are much too busy to bother with such a chore."

Joseph sent his mother a warning look, not liking the direction in which her thoughts were headed. Why would she undermine his efforts to spend time with Lydia knowing he was trying to make things right with her?

Emily just smiled at him and waved Lydia on to change her clothes. Joseph jumped from his seat and knelt down beside his mother, speaking in a perturbed tone.

"What are you doing, Mother? Don't you see I'm trying to win her back and you're putting her in the arms of another man," he voice squeaked to a stop.

Emily's eyes narrowed, and she pinned Joseph down with stern words, "Joseph, I arranged this days ago, and Will made a special effort to clear his time to do this. Besides, don't you have some fences to check or something?"

Emily pushed her chair back and rose to leave the room, but Joseph touched her arm and wondered, "Mother, what are you cooking up this time?"

A smile broke across that woman's face, and she gestured to herself, asking innocently, "Me? Nothing, Joseph, absolutely nothing." Her eyes twinkled as she left the room.

Joseph grumbled under his breath about his mother's choice of teachers. He stood in a doorway of what was left of the stable, grooming Titus and watching Will out of the corner of his eye. He did not like the way the man smiled at Lydia. He did not like the way he patted her on the back and praised her for a good job. And he definitely did not like the way Lydia giggled in response.

Poor Titus never had such a grooming! Joseph brushed and brushed, peeking around the giant steed every time he heard Lydia giggle or Will laugh. The more Joseph heard, the more he growled, and the more he growled, the harder he brushed. In the end, the poor horse suffered until Buck asked Joseph if he was trying to get the black off.

Joseph's smirk made Buck laugh at his boss's obvious jealousy.

"I'm surprised you'd let another man get so close to that pretty little filly of yours, Boss."

Joseph snapped his Stetson off, wiping his sweaty brow and glared in Buck's direction looking pitifully miserable.

"When you got rid of Cutter, you proved you weren't willing to share her. Why are you doing it now?" Buck smiled kindly.

About that time Lydia's laughter floated into the stable and Joseph nearly ran out! He stumbled into the corral, tripping over his own feet, but righted himself before Will or Lydia noticed. Using the lame excuse that Buck needed Will, Joseph dismissed the young cowpoke and faced a smiling Lydia. He pushed his hat back, scratching his head and suddenly feeling like a fool. The smile that was spread across Lydia's face told him he was right.

She stood on the feed bucket in front of him in her riding skirt and white shirtwaist. Her hair was plaited into a single braid like she wore to bed. Joseph's eyes ogled his wife from her boots up to her hair, then dropped to her luscious lips remembering their sweetness and longing to taste them again.

When his eyes locked on hers, he knew that he had been caught, but he was not ashamed. She was his wife, and he loved the way she looked and the way she twisted his heart. He flashed her a lopsided grin and winked, but she was not amused.

She whirled around quickly in a huff but lost her balance on the small feed bucket. Joseph swept her up in his arms to save her from the fall. He held her snugly against his chest, and surely she could feel his heart thundering.

She had instinctively locked her arms around his neck. "Thank you," she breathed. "I'm all right now, you can let go of me."

Joseph thought for long moments about releasing her, but he was enjoying having his wife in his arms. She wiggled around until he eased his hold and set her down, making sure that she was balanced on the righted feed bucket before he completely let her go.

"Lydia, please give me a chance," he whispered close to her ear.

She turned away from him and stared across the ranch land. "You had your chance, Joseph," she reminded him sadly. "I don't know if my heart could stand giving you another."

He closed his eyes and breathed deeply, fearing that she would never forgive him. He twisted her back around to face him and told her that he knew he had made a mess of things, but he wanted to make it right.

Lydia listened, but her face showed the doubt she had.

"Joseph, I just want to learn to ride. If you don't want to teach me, I'll ask Will to come back."

"No!" he countered quickly. "I don't need anyone else to teach my wife to ride."

At Joseph's reference to his *wife*, Lydia cocked her head to one side, squinting an eye uncertain of the game Joseph was playing now.

He smiled innocently at her puzzled stare and winked, causing her to turn a lovely shade of pink. He laughed at her and told her to mount the horse. But her head was a muddle of thoughts, and she completely forgot the things Will had told her.

Joseph mistook her hesitancy for stubbornness and spoke into the back of her head, "Lydia, I know you know how to do this, so get up on that horse."

She whipped her head around and quipped, "How do you know, Joseph?" She glanced up in the direction from which Joseph had first appeared and saw Titus standing in the doorway.

Joseph followed her gaze and saw what she saw; he winced sure he would be in trouble.

"Lydia, honey, I can ex-explain," he said, stuttering to a stop.

She glared at him and accused him of spying on her. He mumbled something about grooming his horse but wished he had kept his mouth shut.

"You were watching me, Joseph. Don't you trust me?" she spit out, resting her fists on her slim hips. "Oh, I get it now, I'm not good enough for you, but no one else can have me either!"

Jumping down from the bucket, she stomped toward the house, but he was tired of her refusal to let him defend himself. In several strides, he was behind her and followed her into the house. She tried to get the bedroom door closed before he came through, but she was no match for him, and he entered easily.

"Now Lydia, you're gonna listen to what I have to say even if I have to wrestle you to the ground."

She glared at him. "Don't you bully me, Joseph Banister. I heard what you told your mother last night. I know that you don't want me here, and believe me, I don't want to be here anymore either."

"What are you talking about? What did you hear last night?"

Lydia refused to answer him. She swiped away some stray tears just before Joseph pulled her into his arms.

"Honey, I don't want to fight, not now or ever again." He raised her chin with his finger and dropped a soft kiss to her lips. As he lingered, his kiss grew more intense and scared Lydia.

She pushed him away. "Stop, Joseph, I don't know whether you are sincere or pretending. But until I do, I think it is best if you move into the guest room."

"What?" he raised his voice, agitated that she accused him of being insincere. "No, Lydia, this is our bedroom, and you are my wife." He crossed his arms standing his ground.

"Joseph, I'm not going to share this room with you any longer."

Joseph's temper had been put to the test, but he failed. He blew up right there and told Lydia that she would share his bed or else! When she shook her head *no*, he stormed from the room.

Sadly, Lydia spoke to a now empty room, "Joseph, I won't be here when you get back."

26

As Joseph stalked across the patio, he never noticed his mother sitting at the corner table crying. She had not meant to be eavesdropping, but it had been hard not to hear the couple fighting.

If only she had not tried to make him jealous, if only she had just let the Lord handle things, but she didn't, and now things were in a worse mess than they had been before.

When she got up to leave the table, she heard the hoof beats of a horse, probably Titus wildly galloping out of the yard. She wiped away more tears and walked toward the door to the living room when Lydia's call stopped her.

"Oh, Mama," she cried and flew into Emily's waiting arms.

"I'm so sorry, Lydia," Emily's voice was full of tears as they stood embracing each other. "I should have never interfered. It's all my fault."

Lydia pulled away just a little so she could see her mother-in-law. "No, Mama, I … I should have tr-tried to listen," she stuttered with tears falling freely.

Emily guided Lydia into the living room, and they sat down on the couch.

"Lydia, do you love Joseph?"

"I don't kn-know anymore," she answered honestly, trying to gain some control. "At one time I … I thought I did, but … but now I'm not sure who the real Joseph is. Sometimes he is sweet and loving and other times he is cold and uncaring." She wiped away more tears and looked to his mother for answers.

"Well, I can tell you that Joseph has not been himself for quite a while. He told me last night that the fear that he felt over this curse thing drove him to the decision not to marry." She prayed she was getting all this right since it all seemed so unreal to her.

"Then I surprised him with you. Little did we know you were a gift from heaven," she said, smiling; she patted Lydia's hand before going on. "You see, he told me last night that he fell in love with you from the start but had to fight it because of the ridiculous plan he had conceived."

"He did?" Lydia interrupted. "I never heard that."

Now it was Emily's turn to be surprised. "You heard us talking?"

Lydia nodded her head and confessed she had heard Joseph's harsh words about never wanting a wife and stopping the whole thing. Emily shook her head and explained that she had heard only the beginning of the conversation and had she continued to listen she would have heard how much he truly loved her and wanted to make their marriage work.

Lydia loved Emily almost as much as her own mother, but she was not sure whether Joseph had told his mother what she wanted to hear or if he told her the truth. She explained to Emily that she was confused about the matter and was going to stay in town. That if Joseph truly loved her, as she said he did, he would come after her, but if not she would earn enough money to go back to St. Louis.

Emily opened her mouth to try to talk Lydia out of her decision but decided to leave it in the Lord's hands this time.

Joseph headed Titus into the stables at sunset. He had been to the rock to pray, not only the piece of ground but to the Lord Jesus his *rock*. He asked for forgiveness and wisdom about Lydia. He admitted that she had changed his whole life and he loved her deeply, longing for a real marriage. He asked the Lord to guide him in winning her back. When he left the *rock*, there was a peace that the Lord was going to make things right, but it lasted only for a short time.

Joseph was about to find out that the patience he had longed for earlier that morning would come at a high cost: tribulation.

He walked through the house with no signs of a soul anywhere. He went into their bedroom and noticed Lydia's things were gone from the dresser. Rushing to the wardrobe, he threw it open and stood in a daze staring at an empty space where her clothes had just been.

"She's gone, Joseph."

While still holding the wardrobe door, he turned to find his mother in the bedroom doorway with red swollen eyes.

How can this be, Lord? I was sure You gave me peace that things were going to work. And my Lydia's gone. Joseph stepped back and lowered himself to the end of the bed. His chest tightened until he felt he wouldn't be able to breathe.

Turning eyes full of misery to his mother, he confessed, "We had a fight."

She silently came to his side and told him she had heard all of it, with a voice thick with tears. She hurried on to tell him about her conversation with Lydia after he left and where she had gone, encouraging him to go after her.

But Joseph was not ready to put off his anger; he was not ready to humble himself and go after his wife. He chose to ignore his mother's plea. Emily could see his decision immediately transform his face. It was that stubbornness that he had as a child.

"Joseph Banister," she scolded, "you're not going after her, are you?"

He shook his head and crossed his arms over his chest.

"No, I can see you have made up your mind, but just you remember," she warned him before she left the room, "you've made your bed!"

Thursday morning, Lydia left her hotel room and applied for a waitress position in the dining room of the Clayton House, which she got and started immediately. One of her first customers was a surprised sheriff.

Spencer Atwater said he would have loved to invite her to join him for breakfast and tell him what had happened, but Lydia's position didn't afford her the privilege. Lydia guessed he would find out soon enough when he made a visit to the Circle B and Emily.

Lydia's day passed in flurry of activity, and by night's end she was exhausted. Throughout the day, she had kept her eyes on the door, hoping to see Joseph, but he never came. As her head settled on her pillow, she prayed Joseph would come for her.

Joseph's day had been no better. He missed Lydia terribly, but his foolish pride would not allow him to go after her. His mother accused him of being just like the pharaoh in Exodus. She reminded him that the Lord had sent the plague of frogs to Egypt, completely covering the land with the slimy creatures. Finally the pharaoh asked Moses to entreat the Lord to take the frogs away, but when Moses asked him when he wanted it done, the pharaoh told him the next morning. Emily told Joseph that the pharaoh wanted one more night with the frogs, and it seemed to her that Joseph wanted one more night with the frogs in that bed that he had made for himself.

Joseph tossed and turned in that bed all night, and by Friday morning, he was an unbearable grouch. Emily and the men of the Circle B steered clear of him. Everyone that knew the couple prayed the Lord would soon bring them back together.

Lydia slowly made her way to the mercantile. She felt as if she had worked a week, but it had only been one day. She groaned within herself. Would Joseph come for her? Would she have to keep working until she had the money to go back to St. Louis? She had no clear direction from the Lord on what she should do.

"I guess I'll stay the course until I hear otherwise," she mumbled.

She didn't noticed Spencer until he joined her on the board-walk. He offered the usual small talk about the day, but Lydia interrupted him with a question.

"Spencer, did Joseph ask you to talk to me?"

He explained that he had gotten the story from a tearful Emily the night before, and he had promised her he would speak to Lydia, while Emily hoped to speak to Joseph.

Although Lydia was disappointed it had not been Joseph, she was not surprised. Spencer assured her that he and Emily were praying for the two of them. He took several moments to encourage her to go back to the ranch and make things right with her husband, but Lydia was convinced that Joseph needed to come to her.

"Besides that," she went on to explain to the sheriff, "I'm not sure I know who Joseph really is or how he will treat me if I do go back."

Spencer said he appreciated her honesty and guided her to a bench in front of his office. "When I was a young man thinking of marrying, my Pa took me aside one day and gave me some of the best advice I'd ever received. He told me to look at the way a young woman treated her father and you'd have a good idea how she would treat you. Now I know in your case that you'd reverse that, but I want you to think about it. How does Joseph treat his mother?"

He watched as Lydia thought about the love and kindness that Joseph had always shown Emily, the way that he was willing to give up his own happiness to ensure that she was happy.

When he saw that Lydia was beginning to understand, he added, "That's the way he would treat you." He patted her hand and entered his office, leaving her alone to think.

Joseph avoided his mother at every turn. He stalked around the ranch sullen and growled if anyone mentioned Lydia's name. Never had those of the Circle B seen him in such a tizzy. Prayers for him and Lydia were more fervent and frequent.

After another night alone, Joseph tried to accept the fact that Lydia was gone for good, but when Joseph saw his miserable reflection in the mirror, he knew life would not be worth living without her.

Saturday passed quickly, the day filled with hard work. Joseph ran the fence line and worked beside Shorty repairing the downed wire. They spoke easily, and Joseph even asked Shorty exactly what he did to court his Susie.

By Sunday morning, Joseph was tired of being alone. He missed Lydia, and he wanted her home. But the *how* was harder to figure out. He spent time before breakfast apologizing to his mother and the ranch hands about his foul mood, then left for church, praying the Lord would speak to his heart.

Joseph searched for Lydia until the service started, then gave up as the service began. Spencer had told him she was still in town, and he prayed that he had not waited too late but promised himself that he would go all the way to St. Louis to get her back.

Joseph's attention was drawn back to the preacher as he began his message, never seeing Lydia slip into the pew just inside the door or the way she watched him during the service.

Preacher Henley explained that his thoughts had been on the story of Moses all week and he could not get away from it. He wondered what kind of a man Moses had been that God would choose him to be the instrument He used to deliver His people from Egyptian bondage and entrust them into his care while they traveled to their promised land.

"Let's look at the choices Moses made, and perhaps we will see why the Lord used him. Throughout his life he was given choices, just as we are, and each time, he chose to honor the Lord.

"Hebrews 11 verses 24 through 26 will help us understand what I mean: 'By faith Moses, when he was come to years, refused to be called the son of Pharaoh's daughter; Choosing rather to suffer affliction with the people of God, than to enjoy the pleasures of sin for a season; Esteeming the reproach of Christ greater riches than the treasures in Egypt: for he had respect unto the recompense of the reward.'

"One choice in his life came when Moses was a young man and had it all. He lived in the palace as a prince and perhaps was in line for the throne, but one day, he realized that all of those things meant nothing to him when compared to the riches of the Lord. When faced with a choice, Moses chose to be with the Lord and His people, even if that meant affliction.

"He faced many such choices in his life from believing the Lord at the burning bush to obeying Him in the wilderness. The Lord honored Moses for his choices and blessed his life. And today we remember him as one of the greatest men in the Bible.

"The people of Israel were faced with an important choice soon after they left Egypt. They came to Kadesh-Barnea, and Moses sent twelve spies to search out the land God had promised them and come back with a report for the people. Ten of the spies feared the giants of the land and gave an evil report to the people. But Caleb and Joshua believed God when He said He would give them the land, and their report encouraged the people to trust the Lord and make the right choice. Sadly, the people chose to believe the evil report of ten men instead of the Word of the Lord, and Israel was doomed to forty years of wandering.

"I said all of this to ask you these questions: What kind of choices are you faced with right now? Will you choose to believe God's Word about your situation or will you wander through life wishing you had?

"Our lives are full of choices between right and wrong, good and evil. The only way we can make the right choices is to make them God's way. We are all faced with decisions in our life, and trusting the Lord and taking Him at His Word is the only way to make the right choices in our life. Go to the Word, and let the Lord speak to your heart from its pages. If you will lean on Him, He will guide your path, but it's your choice. Let's stand and pray."

Lydia quietly slipped out of the church and back to the hotel to change for work, but Joseph sat in the seat while the others filed out of the building. He spent most of the afternoon talking to the preacher about the things he needed to put off and put on in his life. After a time of prayer together, Joseph mounted Titus and headed for home. He needed to inform his mother of his plans for the next week and ask her to pray for him.

27

LYDIA'S FEET HURT BEFORE THEY ever touched the floor. She had only been working in the dining room four days, and she dreaded the thought of taking one more order, but she had no choice.

The word *choice* brought back thoughts of the service yesterday. There were other choices she could make, but she firmly believed that she was doing the right thing and prayed Joseph would come. Her heart ached when she saw him in church Sunday, but she still had hope that he would come.

Then she woke up to the reality that Joseph had made no attempt to see her since she left the ranch Wednesday evening and probably never would. She had underestimated how stubborn he could be.

Joseph had set things in order at the ranch, giving out orders with control and confidence. He hooked his carpet bag onto the saddle horn and headed for town.

His first stop was to see Spencer Atwater. His mother told him right before he left that Spencer wanted to speak to him. He was surprised since he had seen the sheriff at the ranch several nights this past week.

The older man greeted Joseph and asked him to take a seat. Joseph had the distinct impression that Spencer was nervous about something; he hoped it was not bad news about Cutter and asked the sheriff as much.

"No, no, Cutter is safely behind bars for the robberies he committed with the Ketchum Gang. The judge threw the book at him when he learned that Cutter killed a man in a small bank outside of Phoenix. In fact, if you never even press charges against him, he will be in prison for the rest of his life."

Joseph blew out a sigh of relief and wondered, "Then what brings me here this morning?"

"Well, I thought that … that is … maybe," Spencer stumbled through words that made no sense at all.

Joseph watched with great curiosity as Spencer squared his shoulders and released a great sigh.

"I thought that I should ask you about taking your mother's hand in marriage," Spencer's words spilled out quickly.

Joseph's smile instantly spread across his face. "Well, Spencer," he drawled, but when Joseph took in the stressful look on that man's face, he had pity. "I don't know of anyone I'd rather have caring for her than you."

It took Spencer several moments to comprehend what Joseph had said, and when he did, he jumped up in relief, laughing as he grabbed Joseph's hand, pumping it. "Really? Great! You had me worried there for a minute." Spencer's words began to flow at full speed. "I know it's awfully quick, but I promise you, Joseph, I have prayed about this, and I love that woman with all my heart."

Spencer would have rambled on for some time had not Joseph interrupted him. "Spencer, I appreciate your asking, and I know that you two love each other very much. I've never seen Mother happier," he confessed, thinking of the way he would catch her humming around the ranch. "But if you will excuse me, I have business to take care of."

Joseph rose to leave, but Spencer stopped him. "Oh business, does that mean you're headed to the bank?"

"No." Joseph smiled at how the older fellow was pumping for information. "I'm not headed to the bank."

Joseph took a step toward the door, and Spencer stopped him again. "So then you must be headed to the mercantile. I heard Evan's was having a sale this week," he inquired with a twinkle in his eye.

Joseph set his black Stetson on his head and grinned. "No, I'm not headed for Evan's Mercantile."

Joseph had his hand on the doorknob when Spencer stopped him for the third time. "Well, now let me see," he milked his chin grinning. "Your business won't take you to the bank or the mercantile, where in the world are you headed, son?"

Joseph shook his head, knowing very well Spencer knew what brought him to town. He laughed and threw up his hands in surrender. "All right, Sheriff, I can see you're not going to let me leave without telling you my business."

Joseph looked into the smiling eyes of Spencer Atwater and declared, "I'm going to the hotel to find my wife, court her, and marry her if she'll have me!" He grabbed open the door and mounted Titus, turning him in the direction of the Clayton House. He thought for sure he had heard Spencer remark as the door closed, "Praise God!"

Joseph got a room for the week and paid the man to see his horse safely to the livery, anxious to check out the new waitress. He threw his bag in the room, never looking around to see if it would be comfortable; straightened his hat in the mirror; and took the steps at top speed back down to the dining room.

His heart skipped a beat when he spotted her. Even though she looked like she was exhausted, to Joseph she was a sweet sight to his lonely eyes. He wished he could scoop her up into his arms and carry her away from this place, but he was not going to bully her this time; he was coming to court her!

He entered the room just as she ducked through the door into the kitchen, and he took a seat at what he prayed was one of her tables. But if he had to, he was willing to pick himself up and move to another table!

————◈❖◈————

When Lydia came through the kitchen door, she spotted him sitting patiently at one of her tables. She was thankful her arms were empty, for she was sure that she would have dropped whatever she would have been carrying. Shaking fingers ran up her neckline securing wayward strands of black hair back into place, she moved toward the table, smoothing her skirt over her hips and tried to still her racing heart.

"May I take your order, sir?" her voice sounded calmer than she felt.

He sat so tall in the seat their eyes were almost level, and for long moments, he just stared into her blue eyes. He flashed her one of his lopsided grins, and her heart fluttered in her chest so loudly she feared Joseph could hear it.

"Hello," he whispered.

"Hello, yourself." She smiled.

"I'm real hungry, do you have any suggestions?"

"Uh-huh," she mumbled, then grabbed a hold of herself, "you might try the special."

The lopsided grin spread into a full smile. "It won't be as special as you, but I guess I'll try it anyway."

"Lemonade?" She smiled, her lashes fluttering slightly as she remembered the wet kisses he gave her in exchange for a glass of the cool liquid.

"Only if you bring it to me." He winked.

She covered the giggle that threatened to slip out and practically skipped to the kitchen, suddenly not a bit tired.

Once inside, she handed his order to the cook and leaned against the wall for support. *He came!* She could hardly believe it, but he was there just as she had prayed he would be.

She fixed his glass of lemonade and took a deep breath before she swung through the door. He smiled brightly, touching her hand as he received the glass from her. The touch sent tingles of pleasure up her arm, and she blushed, which seemed to please him.

"I was wondering if you would consider having supper with me tonight."

She was so excited she couldn't find her tongue, so she just nodded her agreement.

"What time do you get off work?"

She knew this question required an answer and hoped that she did not sound as breathless as she felt. "Five o'clock," she grinned. "I get off at five o'clock."

His eyes caressed her face before he asked, "Could you be ready at six?"

She knew it would be pushing it, but somehow she would be ready. "Yes," she committed herself.

"Good, we'll have a picnic down by the river."

With the clock chiming five, Lydia flew up the hotel steps to her room. She was surprised to find a tub full of hot water and rose-scented bath soap with a note from Joseph. She also found a new lacy white shirtwaist and a black skirt on her bed.

She grabbed up the clothes, pressing them to her and twirling around the room. *He came for me!*

She repeated over and over in her mind. When she stopped, tears of joy trickled down her cheek, and she knelt by the bed to thank the Lord for bringing Joseph to her.

Promptly at six o'clock, she stood at her mirror, admiring her new outfit when the knock at her door made her jump. She had not been expecting anyone, assuming to meet Joseph in the vestibule. A thought flashed through her mind that perhaps they needed her to work. When the knock came again, she took a breath and went to the door.

There stood Joseph in black jeans, a crisp white shirt, and his ever-present black Stetson twisting in his hand, more handsome than she remembered. He handed her a bouquet of wild flowers and told her how wonderful she looked. He offered her his arm and escorted her outside to a rented buggy.

She bashfully thanked him for the lovely clothes, flowers, and bath, remarking about his thoughtfulness.

At the river, he spread a blanket and unpacked the basket of food he had ordered from the hotel. Joseph was attentive to her every need and asked about her job and room. Likewise Lydia asked about his mother, the ranch, and the hands.

After they ate, he suggested a stroll along the riverside to which she accepted. To the young couple, the evening went by too quickly, hating to say their good nights. Once inside the hotel, Joseph showed Lydia to her room, stopping outside the door to say good night. He asked her if she worked tomorrow, taking her hand in his he raised it to his lips and kissed it gently, his eyes never leaving hers. Then he was gone, and she went to bed wondering when she would see him again.

Bright and early the next morning, she watched as Joseph entered the dining room sitting at the same table as yesterday. She was surprised to see that he had come into town so early.

"Good morning, Joseph," she greeted him with a questioning look. "You're in town awfully early."

"I never left."

"You didn't? You stayed in town last night?"

"Yep," he informed her with a twinkle in his eyes, "plan to stay in town all week," winking at her and causing a blush to cover her face.

"You do?"

"Yep, I'm on business of the most important nature."

Her lips formed an *oh*, assuming that she was not the reason he was here. "Would you like to place an order for breakfast?" unable to hide the coolness in her voice.

"Surprise me," he sent her a cheeky grin. "Do you like surprises?"

She gave him a sideways glance. "Yes, I guess so."

"Good!"

He sipped on the coffee she had set down on the table, and she headed for the kitchen but turned around to look at him, wondering what Joseph was talking about. When she did, she noticed he had been staring after her, and he winked when she looked in his direction.

If I didn't know better, I would think that he is flirting with me! The thought left her giddy with excitement until she remembered he was here on business.

After breakfast, Joseph left, promising to see her later. He left her a sizable tip and went to make some purchases. He visited Spencer and told him of his date with Lydia last night, and the older man assured him he would pass the good news along to Emily tonight. Then he went to the Herzstein's Mercantile to see what lovely thing he could buy for Lydia today. He visited with the preacher for a while and checked on Titus.

When he got back to the hotel, he ordered another bath for Lydia, gave the clerk the new button-up boots and stockings he had purchased, and a card to leave. Then he went into the dining room for something cool to drink.

Lydia's face brightened when he entered the dining room, and he smiled back in return. She hurried to the table with a glass of water and watched as he drank it down in several gulps.

"My, my, you must have been a little thirsty."

He set his glass down before he asked, "Have I ever told you how beautiful your eyes are?" his own eyes staring deep into hers.

It shocked Lydia right to her toes; never could she remember a compliment other than about her clothes. She shook her head nervously while a bright blush transformed her face.

"Will you have dinner with me tonight?"

She had never seen this charming side of him, and it left her dizzy feeling. She touched the table with a hand to steady herself, and he took it in his, his touch adding to her discomfort.

His thumb gently caressed her hand as his eyes met hers. "Please say yes," he whispered.

She could only nod her head before slipping her hand out of his. Someone from across the room called for the waitress, and she reluctantly left the table.

The room seemed so hot to Lydia, and her mind was in a muddle. She was sure that if Joseph looked at her like that again, she would faint from dizziness!

Somehow, she made it through his order of pie and coffee, even after he fussed about it not being as good as her pie. He left with the promise to pick her up at six.

Once again, the clock chimed five, and Lydia raced to her room with energy she never knew she had. To her utter surprise, there was another hot bath awaiting her and new boots with stockings. The card was signed: With all my love, Joseph. *Could this really be happening?* The swirling feeling in her heart every time she saw him told her it was happening, but what did it mean?

Lydia answered the door on the first knock, enjoying the way he glanced over her appearance, and smiled. He leaned his shoulder against the doorway and whispered, "You look wonderful. I like the way your hair is fixed, but I like it even better when it is loose, and I can run my fingers through it."

Lydia was totally undone by such a personal compliment remembering how Joseph would brush her hair. When she could speak, she embarrassed herself again. "Thank you, Joseph. I enjoyed your surprises again tonight. The boots fit perfect and the stockings," she blushed at the mention of her under things, but he raised his head back and laughed at her sweet modesty.

"You deserve surprises all the time," he honestly admitted and offered his arm.

They enjoyed a meal in the dining room, Lydia thankful to be waited on, instead of doing the serving. Then they strolled toward the river to walk alongside its edge. Joseph said he worried that he was keeping her out too late and that she was working too hard. Lydia promised she was doing all right, but just knowing Joseph was concerned made her feel cherished.

Joseph escorted her to her room and thanked her for a lovely evening. For long moments, they stood in the hall, speaking only with their eyes. He pulled her close to him with his hands on her arms, then softly kissed her forehead, sending shivers of delight through her.

By Wednesday, Joseph had developed a routine. He saw Lydia for breakfast, asking her to join him for prayer meeting, made his visit to see Spencer and the preacher, made some purchases at Evan's, and ordered a bath for Lydia. Later in the afternoon, he visited the dining room before Lydia left work and found her totally exhausted. He told her that she should stay in and rest tonight, but she insisted on going.

After work, Lydia was thrilled to find another hot bath; however, she lingered too long and when Joseph knocked she was still trying to fasten her boots.

"Lydia?" he called, worry in his voice.

She opened the door slowly and admitted that she wasn't ready. He noticed how tired she was and suggested again that she just rest this evening, but she would not hear of it.

When he found that she was having trouble buttoning her boots, he sat her on the bed and did it for her. When he finished, he placed his hands on the bed on either side of her, lowering his face until it was very close to hers. His eyes moved over her lovely face, and his chest raised as he took a deep breath of her sweet scent.

"You know that you do crazy things to my heart." Winking at her, he pulled her up off the bed and offered his arm to take her to dinner and church afterward.

Lydia was completely swept off her feet with his undivided attention. Thursday and Friday followed the same routine with each evening Lydia enjoying a hot bath and gifts from Joseph.

Thursday evening, they spoke about their childhoods, and Joseph shared with her the things he had been learning about his temper. He confided in her that he had been spending time with Preacher Henley and was beginning to understand how mistaken he had been.

All too soon the evening was over, and Joseph escorted her back to her room and dropped a kiss on her nose as he said good night. As Lydia watched him walk away, she wondered what would happen to them when his business in town was complete. She bit her lip when she considered that it was Thursday night, and he had never mentioned her moving back to the ranch.

Joseph greeted Lydia earlier Friday morning than he had all week, explaining that he was needed at the ranch today but asked her if she would see him tonight. She agreed but worried that all this was coming to an end.

Before Joseph left town, he visited with Spencer and the preacher, made his purchases at the mercantile, and took the gifts back to hotel, arranging for Lydia's bath.

It felt so good to mount his old friend and ride out to the ranch. He missed being home and sleeping in his own bed but knew that Lydia was worth it and so much more. He wondered at how blind he had been and how close he had come to losing her. *Well, I don't have her yet, but tomorrow …* his thoughts brought a wide grin to his face as he entered the fenced-in land that he called home.

Emily was so excited to have him home and looking so happy. They spent half the morning talking over breakfast and discussing the plans for tomorrow. He rode the range after lunch and checked in with Buck for an update on the rebuilding of the stables and about the herd. He reminded Buck of the plans for tomorrow, and the foreman shook Joseph's hand, assuring him all would be ready.

Joseph enjoyed a hot bath himself and dressed for his evening with Lydia. He closed the door on their bedroom with the promise of being in his own bed tomorrow night.

He knocked on Lydia's door at six o'clock and worried when she didn't answer after the third knock. He cracked the door and peeked around the corner, hurrying inside when he found her sound asleep curled up on the bed. He could not help himself when he dropped a soft kiss on her cheek.

Her eyes slowly opened, and she smiled when she saw that Joseph leaned over her.

"Did I fall asleep?"

"Yep, I thought about just watching you sleep, but my stomach got to growling." He grinned innocently.

Still lying in the bed, she reached out to touch his cleanly shaven cheek. "Thank you for all the surprises this week. You have been so sweet."

Joseph had the distinct impression that Lydia was saying good-bye, and it shook him up. "Are you planning on going somewhere, Lydia?"

He turned her head as his lips lowered to claim his wife's lips. Softly, gently he moved his lips over hers, enjoying their sweetness and promising himself that he would enjoy them every day for the rest of their lives.

The kiss was interrupted by a loud growl from his stomach. He raised his eyebrows in surprise, and they both burst into laughter. The evening was perfect. They enjoyed a picnic beside the river and strolled up and down the riverside hand in hand.

She dared to ask if he had finished his business in town, and he said everything looked good and promised to give her the details tomorrow. She mentioned she had the day off, and he asked if he could see her for a late breakfast. Then Joseph escorted her to her room, kissed each cheek, and promised to see her in the morning about nine.

Lydia woke with a mixture of excitement and fear. She skipped around the room with the giddy excitement of spending the day with her Joseph, and without warning, fear gripped her heart thinking that he would not ask her to come back home.

She picked the pink gingham, knowing it was Joseph's favorite, and took special care with her hair fixing it the way Emily had the day she married Joseph.

Breakfast was delicious, and afterward Joseph took her for a buggy ride ending at the river. Joseph parked the buggy and spread a blanket under a shade tree. He easily lifted Lydia out of the buggy and gestured her toward the blanket.

Her heart fluttered when he took her hands in his. "Lydia, do you remember in the beginning of the week that I told you my business was of the most important nature."

She nodded wide eyed with curiosity, wondering where this was going.

"Honey, making things right with you is the most important business I have right now. I wanted to prove to you that I am not that moody, selfish man you lived with at the Circle B."

Lydia gazed into his eyes, seeing all the love he was trying to tell her about. Smiling, she caressed his cheek.

"Sweetheart, I love you so much, and I don't want to live without you."

"Oh, Joseph," she laughed with tears slipping down her cheeks. "I love you too." She jumped into his arms, knocking him to the ground.

Lying flat on his back with Lydia covering his chest, he wondered, "Does that mean that you will marry me for real?"

She pushed herself up by planting her hands on his chest, "What?"

He locked her in his embrace as he sat up, smiling into her crystal blue eyes. He set her down beside him and got up on his knees. Taking her hand in his, he whispered, "Lydia Banister, will you marry me today, not because my mother sent for you, not because of some ridiculous plan I cooked up, but because I love you and need you in my life as much as I need my very breath."

Lydia went to her room to change her clothes, hoping her tears would dry up before she married Joseph again. She was so surprised to find the room full of flowers and her wedding gown draped across the bed. And there under her dress she found the most feminine, lacy underthings she had ever seen. Her face blushed as her fingers glided over the silky things. There was a small card propped against the pillow that read: *To Lydia, the most precious gift with which I have ever been blessed. All my love, for all my life, Joseph.*

A knock at her door brought Emily into the room, and the women hugged and wept together until Emily threatened that they would be late if they didn't stop the blubbering.

Later as Lydia walked down the aisle of the church, she saw Spencer and all the ranch hands from the Circle B, including Shorty and Susie.

When she reached the altar, Joseph took her hand in his, and she whispered to him, "You had this all planned, didn't you?"

He nodded. "Yep, plans work out the way they should when you consult with the Lord." He winked and flashed her a lopsided grin.

She gasped, "Oh Joseph, what will I do about my job at the hotel?"

"What job? I gave your notice first thing Monday morning before I ever saw you. I told them that come Saturday her place would be beside her husband."

The end.

About the Author

BONNIE HAS BEEN A CHRISTIAN for over forty years. She met her husband, Wayne, while they attended Bible college and have been married for thirty-five years. She and her husband enjoy living and working in the Northern Shenandoah Valley. They have four sons, four wonderful daughters-in-law, and seven precious grandchildren. They are blessed to all live in the same area and attend and serve at the same church. She loves teaching a ladies Sunday school class and working as the church secretary. Her hobbies include reading, writing, sewing, scrapbooking, and crafts.